'Have **[...]** leaving
him?'

'Oh, n**[...]**

'No,' Michael said, 'I don't suppose you
could. . . The job here is almost completed. I'll
be moving on. If I don't see you before I go, I
want you to promise me one thing.' His voice
took on a harsh note. 'Promise me you'll give
up this martyr role your husband had cast you
in. I can see why you feel you must stay married
to him, but for God's sake, Lelia, quit letting
him feed off you.'

Dear Reader

As spring leads into summer, many people's thoughts turn to holidays. This is an ideal time to look out for our holiday reading pack featuring four exciting stories—all set in the beautiful British countryside. The Yorkshire moors, Scotland, the Isle of Wight and Cornwall will be the glorious background to these four wonderfully romantic tales. Let us know what you think of them, and of stories set in the UK in general. Would you like more of them, or do you prefer more exotic climates? Do tell.

The Editor

Rosemary Hammond grew up in California, but has since lived in several other states. Rosemary and her husband have travelled extensively throughout the United States, Mexico, the Caribbean and Canada, both with and without their two sons. She enjoys gardening, music and needlework, but her greatest pleasure has always been reading. She started writing romances because she enjoyed them, but also because the mechanics of fiction fascinated her and she thought they might be something she could do.

Recent titles by the same author:

BARRIER TO LOVE

THE HOUSE ON CHARTRES STREET

BY

ROSEMARY HAMMOND

MILLS & BOON LIMITED
ETON HOUSE 18–24 PARADISE ROAD
RICHMOND SURREY TW9 1SR

First published in Great Britain 1985
by Mills & Boon Limited

© Rosemary Hammond 1985

Australian copyright 1985
Philippine copyright 1992
This edition 1992

ISBN 0 263 77612 3

Set in Plantin 10 on 12 pt.
01-9207-47698

Typeset in Great Britain by County Typesetters, Kent

Made and printed in Great Britain

CHAPTER ONE

THE FIRST time Lelia met Michael Fielding she was almost overcome with panic, a sudden irrational fear that threatened to break her habitual iron control.

She and Armand had driven out from the town house on Chartres Street to the plantation on the east bank of the Mississippi River to see how the restoration was coming along. It was a grey day, cool for New Orleans, even in February, and she hoped the two men would attribute the tremor that ran through her slight body, shivering in the suede designer suit, to the temperature and not the state of her nerves.

When they drove up, he was standing on the wide portico of the graceful mansion directing the workmen. His back was to them, and her first thought was that he was too much of everything. Too tall, too rugged-looking with his worn black jeans and heavy grey pullover. Too physically overpowering with his broad shoulders, his large hands resting on slim hips, long legs apart. As they came closer, she thought that his black hair, curling slightly over the nape of his neck and around his ears, was too long. When he turned, his piercing eyes were too blue, his features too even, the set of his jaw too domineering and authoritative.

He hadn't shaved, and the faint dark stubble on his jaws and upper lip made him seem even rougher and more dangerous. Then he spoke, and she recovered herself,

5

realised that he was only a man, in her husband's employ. How could he be a threat to her?

'Mr Duval,' he called. 'Good morning. Come to see how the work is progressing?'

He gave her a brief, polite look out of those dazzling eyes and took a step forward. His manner was courteous, even diffident, but as he walked towards them, Lelia felt again the odd sensation of danger.

'Good morning, Mr Fielding,' Armand was saying. 'You see I've brought my wife with me this time.' He looked up at Lelia from the wheelchair beside her. 'Darling, this is Michael Fielding, the great man himself, who is going to restore Beaux Champs to its original splendour.' Beaux Champs—Beautiful Fields.

His voice was too pleasant. Although the words themselves were innocuous, he seemed to be issuing some sort of sly challenge. To her? Lelia wondered. Or to the formidable Michael Fielding?

She saw the tall man glance down at Armand, then the blue gaze shifted to her. She lifted her chin slightly, made her face expressionless, and met his gaze.

'How do you do, Mr Fielding.' Her voice was cool, controlled. 'Armand tells me you're working miracles here.'

He only shrugged, the heavy muscles of his chest and arms moving lithely under the grey sweater. Then he nodded politely. 'Mrs Duval,' he said, and shifted his gaze back to Armand.

'Would you like a tour?'

As she followed the two men into the house, Lelia wondered again why Armand had wanted her to come with him this morning. Certainly not for her approval.

He wasn't interested in her opinions. And what was the meaning of that look he had given her just now when he introduced her to Michael Fielding? Thoughtful, appraising, it was as though he was playing with her, trying to penetrate her defences, the cool façade she had so carefully erected.

As she walked unseeing through the immense rooms, the priceless antique furniture and carpets covered with dust sheets, she thought back to the conversation at the breakfast table that morning.

'I want you to come with me to Beaux Champs this morning,' Armand had said.

Lelia looked at him. He always went alone to the family plantation to check on the progress of the restoration, and she wondered why he wanted her with him today. However, she was not in the habit of questioning Armand's wishes.

'Of course,' she replied, setting down the fragile eggshell coffee cup in its saucer. 'What time do you want to leave?'

'As soon as you're dressed.' He thought a moment. 'Wear the new cream suede suit. It will be chilly. The colour suits that dusky skin of yours.'

She pushed the graceful Louis XV chair back from the long mahogany table and stood up, the swirling folds of her white velvet *peignoir* falling around her ankles.

Armand raised a hand. 'Finish your breakfast first. There's no hurry.'

Although they ate their dinner every evening in the elegant, high-ceilinged dining room with Blanche and Tante Amalie, breakfast and lunch were more informal affairs. This morning they were alone in the room.

'I've finished,' she said. Half a croissant, juice, and two cups of the thick, black New Orleans coffee diluted with heavy cream was all she ever had for breakfast. 'I'll just go bathe and dress. I won't be an hour.'

She hesitated, stared down at the patterned Aubusson rug for a moment, then raised her dark eyes to meet his limpid gaze. The brown eyes were petulant, self-pitying. 'Do you need help?' She didn't dare even glance at his wheelchair.

'No,' he said with a frown. He looked away. 'I may not be good for much, but I can still get from the dining room to my bedroom.' His tone was bitter.

She nodded and started towards the door. 'Shall I drive?'

He sighed wearily. 'No. Peter will take us in the Rolls. It needs to be run more often, and I know you don't like to drive it.'

She started to protest that she had never said that, but decided it would only lead to another long harangue about her shortcomings. If Armand chose to treat her like a fragile doll, an incompetent child, that was his privilege.

She walked down the hall to her own bedroom, oppressive with its heavy blue damask draperies, rose-patterned rug and overstuffed antique chairs. She supposed it was a beautiful room, but it never felt as though it belonged to her.

The Duval house was one of the few private residences left in the old French Quarter—the Vieux Carré—of New Orleans. Like the plantation, Beaux Champs, on the Mississippi River, it had been in the Duval family for generations.

The Duvals, like the other old Creole families, were of the aristocracy of New Orleans society. Armand, as one of the wealthiest, the last scion of the oldest family, was adamant that their homes be kept up faithfully in all their original splendour. They were like beautiful works of art, Lelia often thought, but hardly homelike.

She bathed in the scented water of the marble tub, creamed her body, powdered, and put on the lacy hand-made lingerie that Armand insisted she wear. Then she sat at the satin flounced dressing table with its ormolu gilt mirror to arrange her hair and make up her face.

She had her hair done twice a week, and between the visits of the French hairdresser to the house, she only had to smooth out and neaten the heavy black mass, tortured into the elaborate coiffure Armand preferred. She tucked a wayward strand under the intricate arrangement at the top of her head and lightly ran a wire brush over the smooth wings that framed her small dark face.

The make-up was simple. Even though Armand wanted her to look her role of pampered doll to perfection at all times, he abhorred vulgarity. Her smooth, creamy skin needed no heavy layer of powder or paint, but she had little natural colour, and a light blusher, a pale lipstick, a darkening of the eyebrows, were essential for the image he wanted her to project.

She went to the closet to get out the suede suit, and idly wondered what blouse, what scarf, what jewellery to wear with it. She didn't really care. She would have preferred faded jeans and a sweatshirt, her hair cut shorter, hanging loose, no make-up at all.

But, she reminded herself, what she wanted didn't

matter. Armand's wishes were all that counted. Obeying his every demand, indulging his every whim was the only way she could keep the terrible load of guilt she carried in her heart from consuming her.

There was a knock on the door. Armand wheeled in, dressed impeccably, as always, in a tan suit that just matched his carefully cut and combed blond hair, his useless legs resting on the metal step of his chair.

He had, of course, told her what blouse, what scarf, even what shoes, bag and perfume to wear. He had surveyed her critically while she stood there like an obedient child, every inch the sophisticated, well-bred wife of the lord of the manor, until he pronounced himself satisfied, and they were ready to go.

Now, as she lagged behind the two men, barely listening to the technical discussion between them about cornices and pilasters and carvings, she wondered again at Armand's motive in bringing her here.

Since the accident, five years ago, the workings of her husband's mind had been a mystery to Lelia. After he had regained consciousness and discovered he would never walk again, would be paralysed from the waist down for the rest of his life, a shutter had come down over his eyes, and Lelia had been irrevocably shut out, left alone with her guilt.

Once she had realised that her whole life would be spent doing penance for that one foolish, fatal mistake, that she and Armand would never have a marriage in any sense of the word, she had simply withdrawn.

They were in the larger of the two ornate drawing rooms on the main floor now, and Lelia's meditations were interrupted by the sound of voices raised in anger.

'No,' she heard Armand say in the familiar, high-pitched, imperious tone. 'I won't even discuss it.'

Then Michael Fielding's voice, deeper, but with its own hard certainty and authority. 'Just take a look at the architect's drawings if you won't take my word for it. You'll see that the original woodwork on all the fireplaces was natural pecan. One of your ancestors at the end of the last century indulged himself in a renovation of sorts, but that's a far cry from a faithful restoration.'

Then she heard Armand's stubborn voice. 'The fireplaces have always been painted the same colour as the walls, and that's the way they'll stay.'

'Let me explain something to you about. . .'

'No!' The word exploded and echoed in the large room. 'No,' Armand repeated in a sullen tone.

Lelia glanced at them out of the corner of her eye. The dark-haired man was squatting down in front of the fireplace beside Armand's wheelchair, a drawing in his hand, pointing at it. Armand's back was to her, but she could imagine the look on his face, the same look he always got when he was crossed. She watched Michael Fielding and was just close enough to see a muscle twitching along the hard line of his firm jaw.

He stood up now, carefully rolled up the drawing and set it on the mantelpiece. His eyes were half-shut, his face blank.

'Very well, Mr Duval,' he said in an even tone. 'Then I'll have to leave. You hired me for my expert advice, not to cater to your whims. I can't work under those conditions. I never have, and I never will.'

There was silence in the room. Lelia scarcely dared breathe. Why was he doing this? What difference did it make to Michael Fielding how the fireplaces were finished? Upsetting Armand would only make it more difficult for her to live with him. She clenched her fists, hating him for this arrogant insistence on his own way.

'You can't leave now,' Armand said at last in a sulky tone. 'The house is all torn apart.'

'I'll be happy to recommend three or four other men who will be more—accommodating,' was the smooth reply.

There was another long silence. Then Armand wheeled his chair around and glared at Lelia, still standing rigid at the doorway.

'Oh, very well,' he said. 'Have it your own way.'

Lelia expelled a sigh of relief. Without a glance at her, Michael Fielding followed Armand out of the room and the two men continued their tour. She stood staring out of the window, sorry she'd come, wishing they'd hurry, resenting the overbearing man for upsetting Armand.

Then she heard them in the foyer, and it sounded as though they were at it again. Fielding was speaking, his tone reasonable enough, but firm.

'This is the twentieth century, Mr Duval, not the eighteenth. Beaux Champs is a home, not a museum. If you don't take advantage of this opportunity to modernise, while the house is torn apart anyway, it'll never come again.'

'Not five minutes ago, Mr Fielding,' Armand said, 'you were threatening to quit rather than alter its museum-like qualities.'

They had come into the drawing room. The tall man stood with his arms crossed in front of him, leaning back against a wall.

'The purely decorative rooms are one thing,' he explained with elaborate patience. 'To restore them, you must treat them as works of art, museum pieces, if you will. The functional rooms are an entirely different matter. In its original design there were no bathrooms *per se* at Beaux Champs, and the kitchen was in a separate building out at the back of the house.'

'I don't want to talk about it any more,' Armand said loudly.

'I could put in central heating, modernise the kitchen area and baths, put in a lift,' the tall man went on insistently. 'No one would ever know it was there.'

'*I* would know.' Armand was shouting now, almost hysterical.

Lelia looked away, concentrated her gaze on the pink marble fireplace. Central heating, she thought wistfully, recalling the cold winter mornings in the draughty rooms. A modern bathroom, and even though she rarely got the chance to cook, a good stove. And a lift for Armand so he wouldn't have to be carried up and down the wide, curving staircase. But she didn't say anything.

There was total silence in the room now except for the sounds of the workmen coming from the portico out in front and Armand's laboured breathing. She thought of his heart, weakened by the stress of the accident, the surgery, the years of inactivity—all her fault—and wanted to go to him, to calm him, to tell the heartless Mr Fielding to leave him alone. But she didn't dare. She stayed where she was.

Finally, the tall man spoke. His voice was calm, controlled. 'Very well, Mr Duval. It's your house, your money. But since you've brought her, I'd like to hear Mrs Duval's opinion.'

Lelia darted a glance at him, momentarily startled and wide-eyed with apprehension. The expression on his fine features was grave, the blue eyes narrowed. He raised heavy eyebrows slightly, sensing the distress she couldn't hide, and she quickly arranged her features in the usual blank mask.

'My husband makes all those decisions,' she said in a calm, bored voice. 'I have no interest in architecture.'

She turned from him then and saw Armand, a look of intense satisfaction on the pale face, a tight smile on the thin lips.

'You see, Mr Fielding,' he said lightly, 'you won't find an ally in Lelia. Such things as appliances and plumbing and heating bore her.' He held out a hand and she went to him. He grasped one of her own perfectly manicured hands and held it to his lips briefly, possessively. 'My wife is meant to be a decorative flower, not a useful servant.'

Armand's possessive gaze was fastened on her and didn't catch the flicker of disdain in Michael Fielding's eyes as he looked her up and down in her designer suit, elaborate coiffure and carefully posed posture. He looked away.

'As you say,' he commented shortly. 'Is there anything more you want to see today? We haven't started work on the upstairs yet.'

'No,' Armand replied. He wheeled his chair around and started out of the room. 'I'm very satisfied with what you're doing,' he called over his shoulder, 'but then I knew you were the best when I hired you.'

Lelia smiled to herself. Hired him, indeed! She recalled how Armand had pleaded for months with the eminent Michael Fielding to come to New Orleans and supervise the restoration of Beaux Champs. He was the top architect in his field and had people clamouring for his services all over the world. Only the last-minute cancellation of a job in Paris had induced him to come here at all.

She glanced at him out of the corner of her eye to see his reaction to Armand's patronising comment, and was surprised to catch a fleeting smile cross his otherwise impassive face. He must be very sure of himself, she thought, very comfortable being Michael Fielding, to dismiss Armand's haughtiness so lightly.

She envied him that quality. Convent-reared, protected and sheltered all her life until her marriage, she had never done anything to bolster her confidence in herself. Now, she would never even have a child. Her life was useless, without meaning; pointless, with no goal in sight, nothing to strive for, hope for. And it would never change.

'Could I offer you a cup of coffee before you go?' Michael Fielding was saying.

She knew he was living in the old servant's quarters at the back of the kitchen while he was working on Beaux Champs. She was curious to see how he lived, and watched her husband to see what he would say.

'Thank you, no.' Armand's tone was cold, dismissive. 'My wife has a hairdresser's appointment this afternoon and a fitting at the dressmaker's. You understand how these things are, Mr Fielding. Very crucial matters for a woman.' He paused for effect, his words and tone clearly implying that Lelia was nothing but an empty-headed, useless parasite.

Which I am, she thought, yet she was annoyed that Armand chose to demonstrate the fact so clearly to this disturbing man. Disturbing? She thought with surprise. Why did he have that effect on her? He had been courteous, distant, and a model of propriety throughout their stay.

'But, then,' she heard Armand's voice continue on, 'you're not married, are you, Mr Fielding?'

'No. I'm not.' The voice was flat, as though he resented this intrusion into his personal affairs.

Armand beckoned to Lelia. 'Come, darling, we must go.'

They went through the house and back out on to the wide portico in front. The entrance was at ground level, and Armand had no difficulty manoeuvering his wheel-chair to the waiting Rolls by himself.

Peter, stiff in his chauffeur's uniform, was there to meet him. He opened the back door, and Armand lifted himself up with his hands braced on the armrests of the chair and shifted his body on to the seat of the car. Peter folded up the collapsible chair and set it in beside him, then walked around to the other side to open the door for Lelia.

Armand rolled down his window and called to Michael Fielding, who stood a few feet from the car watching.

'By the way, Mr Fielding, we're having a dinner party at the house in town on Saturday night. We would be very pleased if you could join us.' His tone was light, deceptively pleasant.

The other man hesitated. Lelia sat rigidly beside her

husband waiting for him to reply, hoping he would refuse. Why had Armand invited him? What game was he playing? She kept her eyes firmly ahead, fixed on the back of Peter's peaked cap, stiff and unmoving.

'Yes,' he finally replied. 'I'd like to come.'

'Good,' Armand said, pleased. 'Seven o'clock. You know the address. It's on Chartres Street in the Vieux Carré. The French Quarter,' he added, as if Fielding were ignorant of the fact.

'Yes,' came the dry reply, 'I know.'

Armand leaned forward and knocked on the glass partition, rolled up his window, and the Rolls moved down the curving drive, its powerful engine purring, past the giant magnolias, dogwood and weeping cypress to the River Road.

They drove along the levee, the vast expanse of the Mississippi River at their right, back towards town. There were other old plantations set back from the road, and many more further inland along the bayous, those winding fingers of water that broke off intermittently from the mighty river.

'Well, my dear,' Armand said to her after a short silence, 'what did you think of Mr Fielding?'

Not, what did you think of the restoration, but what she thought of the man. Why? She turned her calm dark eyes on him.

'He seems competent. It's too soon to tell, isn't it? The work has hardly begun.'

She wondered if he realised she was deliberately misunderstanding him. Apparently not, since he merely gave a small grunt of satisfaction at her reply and didn't pursue the subject.

They had gone to Beaux Champs on a Wednesday, and during the next few days Lelia found herself several times wondering again why Armand had taken her, why he had invited Michael Fielding to the house Saturday night.

She had plenty of time for this. Her life was a boring round of shopping, luncheons, social engagements. It seemed to her sometimes that the most important decision she ever had to make was what to wear to this function or that, and more often than not Armand made that decision for her.

Tante Amalie, Armand's mother and Lelia's own distant cousin, made all the domestic arrangements in the house on Chartres Street, and Blanche, another distant poor relation like Lelia, supervised the housekeeping.

At dinner that Wednesday night, Armand mentioned to Tante Amalie and Blanche that he had taken Lelia out to the plantation that morning.

Tante Amalie, tiny and birdlike, with bright little black eyes, darted a swift look at Lelia, then at Armand.

'What on earth for?' she asked.

Armand frowned. 'Why on earth not is a better question. She is my wife. It is her home, too.'

Lelia watched as Tante made a brief gesture of dismissal. She looks like a small crow, she thought, always dressed in black, always hovering, the sharp eyes flicking everywhere. Nothing escaped her.

Blanche, tall and blonde, sleek and self-assured, gave Armand a reproachful look. 'I'm crushed,' she said lightly, making a joke of it. 'I've asked you repeatedly to take me, Armand.'

'I will, Blanche,' he replied easily, 'as soon as there's

something to see. You have important duties here. You are not as free as Lelia.'

Free! Lelia thought. What a joke! She was as bound and fettered as though she were in prison. She continued picking at her boeuf bourguignon, not speaking, not allowing her thoughts to show on her face.

'Well, of course,' Blanche was saying with a little laugh, 'I realise that as your wife Lelia has certain privileges that don't extend to me.' Her voice was playful. 'But promise me, Armand, you will take me soon.'

'As soon as there's something to see, *chérie*, I promise.'

Lelia pushed her plate away, only half listening to the others' conversation. They were discussing the dinner Saturday night, and would neither ask for not expect her opinion.

Blanche is in love with Armand, she thought, sipping at her glass of fine claret. She always has been. How I wish he'd married her instead! Then the accident would never have happened. Armand would be walking around. They would have children by now. And she would be free.

After dinner, as always, the family had coffee in the drawing room on the main floor. It was a two-storey house and since the accident that crippled Armand, it had been remodelled extensively into two self-contained apartments.

Lelia and Armand occupied the main floor, so that there were no stairs for him to negotiate, and Blanche and Tante Amalie shared the upstairs apartment. All their communal living and entertaining were done on the main floor.

Tant Amalie settled down now to her interminable needlepoint, half-glasses perched on her button nose, while Blanche took up her book. Lelia would have liked to read, but she and Armand always had a game of chess right after dinner.

They sat across from each other now over the inlaid parquet game table, the ivory chessmen gleaming in the light of the crystal chandelier set high on the decorated ceiling. The chairs, more antiques, were spindly and uncomfortable.

Lelia always lost in these nightly games. She was a good player, but had lost the power to concentrate. She cared no more about the chess game than she did about anything else in her barren life.

'You're looking especially beautiful tonight, darling,' Armand murmured as he set up the chessmen.

Lelia darted him a quick glance. She had changed before dinner into a simple dress of pale rust-coloured tissue wool, elegantly cut to emphasise the small firm breasts, the slim waist and curving hips. Every dark hair on her head was arranged perfectly, and her light make-up was impeccable. Clusters of pearls glowed at her ears, the huge diamond engagement ring sparkled on her finger, and her posture in the uncomfortable chair was poised, ladylike, as she had been taught to sit by the sisters at the convent.

'Thank you,' she said. She knew he genuinely admired her looks, always had, even when she first appeared at the house on Chartres Street six years ago, fresh out of the convent in her dark blue uniform, ponytail and awkward manner.

She had been eighteen. Her father, the son of one of

Tante Amalie's distant cousins, had just died, and the strong familial feeling for blood relations among Louisiana Creoles demanded that the Duvals take in the orphaned girl. Her mother had died when she was born, and she was now alone in the world except for them.

She had come expecting only to be taken on as a servant or companion, at best to find employment at the family's textile mill or sugar plantation. The good sisters, while raising her to be a lady, had also insisted that she learn a trade, so that she had come out of the convent knowing not only how to behave in society, play the piano passably and sew fine seams, but also how to type and balance accounts.

Instead, she hadn't been in the house a month when she caught the eye of the only son of the family, Armand Duval, only three years her senior. Handsome and sophisticated, with almost feminine good looks, he had flattered her, pursued her, courted her persistently until she had agreed to marry him.

Tante Amalie had been horrified at first, then later, sensing Lelia's pliable nature, had resigned herself to the marriage. As the last male Duval, Armand had been petted and pampered by his mother to the point where she didn't dare oppose him in anything. And, after all, the girl had Duval blood, knew how to behave, and would pose no threat to her own iron reign over the household.

'It's your move.' Armand's impatient voice broke into her thoughts. 'I swear, Lelia, you get more absent-minded every day. One would think you were eighty instead of only twenty-four.'

Lelia shook herself and tried to pay attention to the

game. She looked down at the pieces and moved her bishop. Armand immediately took it with a pawn.

'You're not even trying,' he complained in a fretful tone.

The room was large, and the chess table was set up at some distance from the other two women. There was music coming from the stereo set. Lelia thought for a moment, then made up her mind to speak, to try once again.

'Armand,' she said in a low voice, 'if you would only give me something to do, perhaps I could learn to use my mind again and wouldn't be so vague.'

'And just what did you have in mind?' he asked lazily.

'I don't know. Anything. Household accounts. Shopping. I know how to cook. Or perhaps you could find something for me to do at the mill.'

'Out of the question.' There was finality in his voice. 'You are my wife. You have a position in society to maintain. I can't allow you to do a servant's work.'

'But, Armand. . .'

'No,' he said more firmly, and she could sense the finality underlying the curt word.

She shrugged. She knew it was hopeless. She looked down at the board again, trying to concentrate. Then Armand spoke again.

'Perhaps what you had in mind was to help Mr Fielding with the restoration at Beaux Champs.' A sly purposefulness was implicit in the casual tone.

She opened her eyes wide, genuinely surprised. 'What in the world could I do there?'

'Oh, I don't know.' His long, aristocratic fingers toyed with the ivory bishop he had taken from her. 'I'm sure he would be delighted to have your assistance. I saw the way he looked at you.'

'You must be joking,' she said with a little laugh. 'If Mr Fielding looked at me at all, I'm sure it was with contempt for such a useless creature.'

'Ah, useless, perhaps, but most ornamental.' He took her hand and brought it to his lips. 'You give your seductive powers too little credit, my darling.' He turned the hand over and kissed the palm. She shivered at his touch.

He dropped her hand abruptly, and the longing expression on his pinched features turned to one of agonised frustration. She drew in her breath sharply. She had put that look there. She was the cause of his torment, the reason he could not be a real husband to her, never had been, never would be.

Lying alone that night in the ornate bed canopied with yards of blue silk, and dressed in yet another exquisite nightgown of lace and satin, Lelia relived the accident in her mind again.

The wedding, one of the important social events of the season, was held at the St Louis Basilica in Jackson Square. Armand had looked so handsome with his pale blond good looks, his slight form quite dashing in the cutaway coat and white tie.

Lelia thought she had been madly in love with him at the time. Now she wasn't so sure. She had barely spoken to a man in her whole life before Armand. She admired him, respected him, was flattered by his attentions, and proud he had chosen her to be his wife.

After the huge reception at Beaux Champs, they had

driven to the airport alone to catch their flight to Paris. It was fall, October, hurricane season, and the curving River Road was awash with the pelting rain. The sky was so dark that Armand had turned on the headlights, and the windscreen wipers barely made a dent in the steady downpour.

Not an auspicious beginning for a honeymoon, Lelia had thought when she awoke that morning to the heavy mass of black thunderclouds and whistling wind. Still, she had been happy, anxious to start her new life as Mrs Armand Duval.

They were just coming around one of the sharper curves of the road when Lelia saw it, a young deer directly ahead of them in the road, frozen rigid, hypnotised by the glare of the headlights and confused by the noise of the storm.

'Stop, Armand!' she had cried, but it was too late to brake on that slippery road. When she saw that he had no intention of stopping, in a moment of panic she grabbed the steering wheel and twisted it. The car left the road, inches from the deer, rolled over several times on the embankment, and came to a grinding halt just at the river's edge.

It was a miracle the accident hadn't killed them both, instead of just crippling Armand for life. He had had a weak heart since childhood, and Lelia was thankful that at least she hadn't murdered her husband through that one thoughtless, foolish act.

She knew she had been wrong, that every authority advised hitting an animal in the road rather than endangering the lives of human beings. All she was aware of at the time were those frightened brown eyes of the little deer. It was no excuse. She had done a terrible thing, had ruined Armand's life, her marriage, the family's hopes for an heir, and she must pay for it.

CHAPTER TWO

AT SEVEN o'clock on Saturday evening, Lelia stood at the entrance to the drawing room with Armand in his chair at her side, greeting their guests as they entered from the long tiled foyer. Tante Amalie and Blanche had seen to all the arrangements, decided what food and wine were to be served, made the seating plan at the long dining table, and had supervised the decorations in the seldom-used small ballroom on the main floor.

The cream of New Orleans society had been invited, the women resplendent in their colourful long dresses, the men elegant in their formal black attire.

'Good evening, Charles,' Armand was saying to a stockily built man with thinning sandy hair.

Lelia turned from the woman she had been speaking to and held out a hand. Charles Donaldson was the family lawyer, an old friend.

'How nice to see you, Charles,' she said inclining her head slightly as she had been taught to do, a practised gracious smile on her lips.

'Lelia,' Charles said, bowing and kissing the proffered hand. It seemed an incongruous gesture coming from him. He looked as though he would be more at home on a football field than a society ballroom. 'You're looking more beautiful than ever.'

She had dressed with her usual care that evening in a very pale greyish-pink dress. Ashes of roses, the dressmaker had called it. It was extremely low-cut, the rounded neckline plunging down to barely cover her high firm breasts, gathered just below them, then falling away in graceful folds like a Grecian gown.

It was another of Armand's choices. She often wondered why a man who was unable to make love to his wife, and who guarded her jealously from other men, insisted on dressing her in the most provocative clothes. It was as though he was proclaiming to the world that this tempting woman was his possession, that even though she would never be entirely his, it pleased him to excite other men to envy.

While Charles and Armand chatted about business, Lelia continued to greet the guests, until finally the steady flow of people ceased. The others had all drifted on past her into the drawing room for drinks, and Lelia stood alone at the doorway.

Michael Fielding hadn't come. She didn't blame him after the way Armand had behaved on Wednesday. It was probably just as well. She felt a decided antipathy towards him, and it was obvious that he disturbed Armand in some mysterious way.

Then, just as she turned to join her guests, she saw him. He was walking towards her down the long hall, alone. She stared at him, and for one heart-stopping moment their eyes met. He stood not ten feet from her, tall and breathtaking in his formal black suit and tie. Tiny agate studs gleamed in his stiff white shirt front. The unruly black hair was combed neatly, his face clean-shaven.

He continued walking towards her in easy, confident strides. She experienced a brief insane impulse to shrink back from him as he approached, and although she recovered herself instantly, her hand still trembled when she held it out to him. He threatened her in some obscure way, and she was sorry Armand had invited him.

'Good evening, Mr Fielding,' she murmured mechanically. 'So glad you could come.'

Her own hand was swallowed up in his large strong one, then dropped. 'I'm sorry I'm late. Last minute flap out at Beaux Champs.'

'Ah, Mr Fielding.' Armand had wheeled back to her side. 'Welcome. Come, let's join the others.'

During dinner at the long dining table and afterwards over bandy and liqueurs back in the drawing room, Lelia's eyes sought out the tall man several times, drawn by a force she didn't begin to comprehend. Regardless of her personal feelings about him, he was a guest in her home, she rationalised and she was well-schooled in the role of hostess. She was merely afraid he would feel out of place, she told herself, and wondered if Armand hadn't invited him for that very reason, as some sort of retribution for the argument they'd had the other day. Armand was not accustomed to opposition, and she knew it had disturbed him.

She soon saw however that she needn't have worried about him. Michael Fielding seemed to be as comfortable in a society drawing room as he was on the job overseeing his workmen. They had moved into the ballroom now for the dancing, and as she glanced at him across the room, she could see that he was in no way intimidated or ill-at-ease.

He was standing at the edge of the dance floor in a small group of people, a drink in his hand, his dark head bent, listening to old Charlotte Valois telling one of her interminable, boring stories. All of a sudden, he straightened up, threw his head back and laughed.

Lelia turned her head away, but not before she saw the covetous looks several of the younger women were casting his way. What fools women were, she thought. Can't they see what a predator he is? Then she dismissed the thought from her mind. What did she care? It was not her affair, after all.

She gripped the back of Armand's chair and leaned down to him.

'Can I get you a drink?' she asked. She had to raise her voice to be heard. Blanche had hired a small orchestra for the evening, and now that the music had started, couples began drifting out on to the dance floor.

Armand shook his head. 'No. I'll get it myself. Here comes Charles. Dance with him.'

She frowned. She rarely danced. Since Armand couldn't do so, she felt it disloyal to him. On the few occasions she had tried it, he seemed quite upset. 'Are you sure?' He nodded.

'Lelia,' Charles said, 'will you dance with me?' He glanced down at Armand, evidently expecting a negative answer.

'Oh, I trust you with my beautiful wife,' Armand said in an ironic tone. 'No offence meant, but as the family lawyer, I don't think you'll risk trying to seduce her.'

Lelia flushed. 'Armand! What a thing to say.' He only glanced up at her, a sly smile on his face.

Charles laughed. 'Don't worry, Armand,' he said lightly. 'Not only am I safe, but everyone knows Lelia is not seducible.'

He held out an arm. Lelia took it and they started to dance sedately. She was stiff in his arms, and he held her at a distance.

'Its a wonderful party, Lelia.' His kind face smiled down at her. 'But, then, your parties always are.'

'Thank Tante Amalie and Blanche for that, Charles.' She smiled woodenly. 'They're the ones responsible.'

He frowned and his hold on her tightened slightly. After a short pause, he said, 'You know, Lelia, it's none of my business, but you really should find something to do with yourself.'

She gave him a quick look. 'Armand prefers it that I don't.' Her voice was expressionless. 'I've asked.'

'I see. Maybe I should speak to Armand, then.'

'No,' she said quickly. 'He would resent any interference in his private life, even from you.' She forced a smile. 'I'm really quite content. Who wouldn't be? I live like a fairy princess, my every desire satisfied.'

He raised an eyebrow. 'Every desire, Lelia?' he asked softly.

She coloured, blinked away a sudden stinging tear, and turned her head away. 'Do you know Mr Fielding?' she asked, hurriedly changing the subject. 'Armand had hired him to restore Beaux Champs.'

'Yes, I know that. He has a fine reputation. I don't know him well personally, but he seems quite pleasant.' He laughed. 'At least the women find him so.'

'Yes, I'd noticed,' she said drily. 'He's a little overwhelming for my taste.'

The music stopped, and Charles began to lead her back to the sidelines. She looked around for Armand, but he had disappeared. Then the orchestra started playing again, a slow tune.

'Please go on and dance,' she said to Charles. 'An attractive young bachelor like you must have his pick of partners. Don't worry about me. I'll just go find Armand.'

Then, as Charles turned away, Michael Fielding was beside her. 'Would you care to dance, Mrs Duval?' he asked politely.

Before the automatic 'No, thank you' reached her lips, she found herself in his arms being propelled out on to the dance floor. To escape him, she would have to make a scene. Michael Fielding was not the kind of man who would take resistance meekly. Then she thought, after all, it was only a dance.

Yet, it was dancing as she had never before experienced it. Unlike Charles, he seemed to have no reservations about holding her quite closely up against his tall, lean body, even uncomfortably so. She tried to pull away from him, but his grip on her hand, his arm around her waist, were firm.

She fought down her growing anger and allowed him to hold her, but she made her body stiff and unyielding. They didn't speak. He hummed lightly under his breath. His steps were firm, and gradually she began to relax, in spite of her disquietude.

He looked down at her, his mouth quirked in a teasing smile. 'That's better,' he said. 'Just go with the music.'

Immediately, she stiffened again, and his eyes narrowed. 'Don't do that,' he muttered sharply under his breath, and pulled her closer.

She could feel the hardness of his strong thighs through the elegant dark trousers as he moved in time to the music. The powerful arm encircling her, the large hand at her waist lying on the thin, clinging material of her dress, made her uncomfortable. Yet, she couldn't resist the sensations of pleasure that began to flow through her, nor the spontaneous pliability of her body as it pressed against his.

'Well, Mrs Duval,' his voice floated down to her, 'did you have another gruelling day at the hairdresser's?' He surveyed the elaborate construction on her head. 'Or was it the dressmaker today?' His eyes shifted down insolently to her breasts, the dark valley between them quite visible in the low-cut dress.

She raised her eyes and gave him a cool look. 'Is my private life really of such momentous concern to you, Mr Fielding?' She was stung by his remark, but didn't want him to know it.

He raised his eyebrows and the blue eyes flashed down at her, boring into her. She held his gaze without flinching.

'Perhaps,' he said at last. His hold on her tightened. He looked away and started humming again.

What did he mean by that remark? As she pondered this, she looked over his shoulder, and saw Armand through the crowd of people on the dance floor. He was sitting in his chair on the sidelines, sipping a drink. Charlotte Valois stood beside him, leaning down, her loud-pitched voice droning.

Although he seemed to be listening to Charlotte, his eyes over the rim of his glass were fixed firmly on Lelia. She couldn't read their expression, but knew instinctively that he was not pleased.

The music stopped. She drew away from Michael

Fielding and started walking away from him towards Armand, wishing she could shake off the hand still holding her bare arm.

'Thank you for the dance, Mrs Duval,' he said gravely when they had reached Armand, 'and for inviting me. I must be going now.'

She saw the two men glance at each other. 'Glad you could come, Fielding,' Armand drawled. He darted an enigmatic look at Lelia, then back to the tall man. 'Tell me, do you agree with Charles Donaldson that my wife is not seducible?'

Lelia wanted to sink through the floor, but she only lifted her chin and made her face impassive. Charlotte Valois burst into shocked laughter.

'Oh, Armand, what a naughty thing to say. Everyone knows our Lelia is purity itself.'

Lelia managed a tight smile. 'How many brandies have you had, Armand?' she asked lightly.

She didn't dare look at Michael Fielding, but in an uncanny way she could sense the anger flowing from him and that he was holding himself as tensely as a wild animal poised for mortal combat.

Then Armand laughed, and the air was cleared. 'You must forgive me my little joke, Mr Fielding,' he said easily. He took Lelia's hand and held it to his lips, his eyes travelling meaningfully down from her perfect coiffure to rest possessively on her breast.

Michael Fielding turned his blue gaze on her, their eyes meeting briefly once again. 'Goodnight, then, Mrs Duval, and thank you again.' His tone was flat, his expression inscrutable. He nodded at Armand, then turned and walked away from them in an easy gait, tall and arrogant as he threaded his way through the crowd.

Late that night, Lelia sat at her dressing table in her elegant bedroom brushing out her hair. The hairdresser would come in the morning to construct another elaborate coiffure, but tonight she wanted to feel the long black strands hanging free down her back over the white dressing gown of fine lawn.

Her mind wandered back over the party. Another success, she thought. Inevitably, almost against her will, the dance with Michael Fielding intruded, and she considered his oddly contradictory attitude towards her. He seemed to disapprove of her, even to mock her useless life, yet at the same time be drawn to her. He was a man, she thought, who was used to having his own way with women. If he found the wife of his employer attractive, he would probably have no compunction at using his seductive power on her.

And there was no denying that power. All the other women at the party were eating him alive with their eyes, and she was grateful for the protection of her married status.

There was a knock on the door. Armand entered and wheeled over so that he was beside her. He gazed at her reflection in the mirror as she continued to brush her hair.

'Are you tired, Armand?' she asked. His face seemed even more pale and drawn tonight.

'No. Why should I be tired?' His voice was abrupt. He reached out a hand and began to stroke the long black hair.

Imperceptibly, she flinched at his touch, hoping he

wouldn't notice. His hand tightened in the thick strands, pulling, twisting.

'Armand!' she cried. 'You're hurting me.'

She looked into the mirror and saw that his lips were trembling. He seemed to be making an effort to control himself, but in the brown eyes was a look of malevolent pleasure.

With a little shock she thought, he enjoys hurting me. She closed her eyes. I want to die, she thought. I give Armand no joy, and I'm as unhappy as he is. Why continue on like this?

His grasp on her hair loosened. She opened her eyes. The evil look was gone, but in its place was a familiar lazy boredom that frightened her even more. She knew she pitied him more than she could say, but couldn't help wondering sometimes if he didn't almost enjoy his self-pity, if he didn't use it as an excuse to get his own way in everything.

Finally, he spoke. 'Did you enjoy your dance with Mr Fielding?' he asked, idly running his fingers through her hair.

'Not especially.'

'He's an attractive man.'

She shrugged. 'I suppose some women would find him so.'

'But not you?'

'I haven't thought about it. His looks don't come into it. He's arrogant and overbearing and too sure of himself.'

'You don't like him, then?'

'Not especially.' It was true. He made her uncomfortable with those penetrating blue eyes and probing questions.

They were silent for some time as she continued to brush her hair.

'I've been thinking over what you said last week, about wanting something to do,' he said at last.

'Yes?' she said uneasily, instantly wary. Armand's kindness usually presaged a subtle attack of some kind.

'I've decided that you can help me after all,' he went on. 'The work is piling up at the mill and demands more of my time and attention. So, I would like you to take on some of the responsibility of overseeing the restoration of Beaux Champs.'

Her eyes widened. She knew this wasn't true. The mill was quite adequately managed by others. Armand was only a figurehead. She turned to him, but his face was closed, his expression unreadable.

'But, what could I do? I don't know anything about it.'

'All you have to do is see that my instructions are carried out to the letter.' He grimaced. 'Mr Fielding has too many innovative ideas to suit me. He's the best in his field, but that doesn't give him the right to countermand my orders. I don't trust him.'

Could it be, she wondered, that Armand is afraid of him and is sending me in his place so that I will be blamed if the man does go ahead against Armand's wishes? She would be caught in the middle.

'Armand, I don't think. . .'

'You said you wanted something to do,' he said, his voice rising petulantly, 'then when I offer you a task that would help me, you back away from it. Why, Lelia?' His hand tightened in her hair again. 'Are you afraid of the formidable Mr Fielding?'

'Of course not. It's just that I don't feel competent. . .' Her voice trailed off.

'I will tell you what I want you to look for. All you have to do is report back to me if he hasn't done exactly what I have specified.' His hand moved to her shoulder, gently kneading it under the thin *peignoir*. 'I need someone I can trust, someone who has only my best interests at heart.'

'Very well, Armand. If you think I can do it.'

'Good,' he said. 'That's settled, then.'

His hand left her shoulder and slid down her arm. Her flesh crawled uncontrollably under his touch, but she forced herself to turn and smile at him.

'Thank you, Armand,' she said. 'I'll try not to disappoint you.'

When he had left, she got into bed and lay in the darkness, thinking. The heavy draperies at the windows muffled the sounds coming from the busy streets of the French Quarter, a popular place for tourists, with its fine restaurants, museums, hotels and many night spots. One could still hear the original Dixieland jazz at several places, and she thought she could hear it dimly now.

She wondered why Armand had asked her to help him supervise the restoration. She wanted to believe he was just being kind, but somehow she doubted it. She didn't trust him. Like a jailer who opens the door of a cell merely to lead a prisoner to execution, he seemed to be offering her freedom, a useful task, with something even worse in store for her at the back of his twisted mind.

Still, she would do her best to satisfy him. Then, suddenly, her heart stopped as it occurred to her that going to Beaux Champs would mean dealing with Michael Fielding. And, of course, Armand was well aware of that fact.

She thought of the remark he had made tonight at the dance about her seducibility, and the way he had looked at her when he saw her on the dance floor in Michael Fielding's arms. It was almost as though he was throwing them together. Why? To punish her, knowing she didn't like the man?

She fought back tears of self-pity. I have much to be grateful for, she reminded herself, far more than I deserve. Armand gives me everything I could ever ask for. Except love, a little voice whispered in her heart. Except freedom.

In the days that followed nothing more was said about her going to Beaux Champs. Lelia didn't know if Armand had been out to the plantation himself or not. He never said. She began to think he had forgotten his promise, or that she had dreamed it.

However, one morning at breakfast a few weeks later, Armand turned to her and told her he wanted her to drive out to Beaux Champs that morning. She was pleased, but somewhat apprehensive.

'Is there anything in particular you want me to do?' she asked.

'Just make sure Fielding hasn't implemented any of his ideas about modernising the place.'

She sipped at her coffee and buttered a croissant, thinking over his remark. 'Surely he wouldn't do that? You made it quite clear you were opposed to it.'

He gave a short dry laugh and pushed his chair back from the table. 'Mr Fielding has the notion that he is a law unto himself,' he remarked in a sulky tone. 'I want to keep an eye on him.'

He wheeled past her, kissed her lightly on the cheek, and said, 'Be careful, Lelia.'

She looked at him. 'What do you mean?'

He waved a hand. 'Oh, nothing. Just that he might try to convince you to oppose my wishes.'

Lelia was shocked. 'Armand, you know he could never do that. No one could.'

He patted her arm and smiled. 'That's my good loyal wife.'

It was a sunny day in mid-March, quite warm, and as Lelia drove up the winding road to Beaux Champs, she could see the first of the early rhododendrons just beginning to burst into bloom.

As she parked the blue Thunderbird and got out of the car, she wondered if Armand had told Mr Fielding she would be coming out that day. Probably not, she thought. He would want it to be a surprise visit.

There was no sign of life on the wide portico, but from inside the house she could hear men's voices, the sound of hammering and sawing. She went inside.

For once, she had chosen her own attire, and was dressed in a simple brown corduroy suit with a cream-coloured silk shirt and brilliant rust and gold paisley scarf. She felt businesslike and efficient in her sensible brown shoes and leather bag, just like a real working woman with a busy, useful life.

Her step was springy as she walked through the downstairs rooms towards the back of the house where the noises were coming from.

They were in the library, and when she opened the

door, she saw Michael Fielding over by the fireplace holding up the black marble mantel, while two workmen in overalls knelt at his feet hammering at a scaffolding. The noise was deafening, and none of the men looked up when she came inside.

Lelia drew in her breath sharply when she saw him, and her newly won confidence began to ebb away. He was dressed in worn dusty blue jeans and nothing else. The trousers hung quite low on his slim hips, and above them his lithe, muscular body, glistening with perspiration, tapered up to a powerfully built chest and broad shoulders. The muscles of his arms bulged under the strain of holding the heavy marble, and the tendons in the long column of his neck stood out.

She waited until they were through, her eyes fastened on the tall form and the shock of untidy dark hair as though hypnotised. Finally, with a grunt, he lowered the marble down carefully on the wooden supports, every muscle tense, then expelled a deep breath and stood up straight. He flexed his arms, wiped his hands on the legs of the jeans, then turned and saw her.

She dropped her eyes quickly from that dazzling blue gaze and began to walk towards him.

'Good morning,' she said politely. 'I hope I'm not interrupting. My husband asked me to come out to check on your progress. He couldn't come himself.'

Her voice faltered. The three men only stared at her, and she began to feel self-conscious, as though she had no business here.

'Good morning, Mrs Duval,' the tall man said finally. He reached behind him and grabbed a paint-stained white shirt from a wooden chair, slipped it on, and slowly began buttoning it. 'What is it you would like to—check on—first?'

He resents my coming, she thought, and for a moment she was tempted to turn and run out of the room. The sheer physical presence of the man disturbed her. Even though the shirt was firmly buttoned now, she couldn't help remembering what was underneath. She watched as he tucked it neatly into the waistband of his jeans.

Then she thought, I am not going to let this man intimidate me. She lifted her chin and gave him a haughty look. This is my husband's house, she wanted to convey to him by the gesture, and I am here because he sent me, because I have every right to be here.

'Shall we start with the kitchen?' Her voice was cool and composed.

He nodded curtly, turned and gave brief instructions to the two workmen, still kneeling on the floor, then followed her out of the room.

They walked in silence out into the wide entrance hall, past the curving staircase, and down through a long narrower hall that led to the back of the house. Everything—carpets, furniture, paintings, light fixtures—was covered with the canvas dust sheets.

It looks like a ghost house, she thought, but then she had never really felt at home here. It was more a museum than a place to live in, with its sixteen-foot ceilings, ornate decoration and priceless furnishings. She much preferred the smaller house on Chartres Street, for all its clutter of overstuffed chairs and heavy drapery.

'What in particular did you want to see?' he asked her now.

They had come to the kitchen, a large room with an

enormous wood-burning black stove, a large marble-topped table in the centre, and vast cupboards lining the walls.

She marched past him confidently, without a glance, her head held high. She looked around the room. There was no sign of the suspected modernisation. A pity, she couldn't help thinking, but Armand's wishes were law. Everything seemed in order.

'We've started on the upstairs bathrooms,' he said from behind her in his deep voice. 'I'm sure Mr Duval will expect a report on those as well.'

She whirled around, alert to the sarcasm in his voice. He knew she had come because Armand didn't trust him.

'Very well,' she said.

Something in his arrogant stance, his coolly appraising look, angered her, made her want to lash out at him, assert her authority.

'As you pointed out the other day, Mr Fielding, it is my husband's house, his money.' Her voice was sharp, cutting.

'That's right,' he said calmly. 'And we both know he gets full value for what he pays for, don't we, Mrs Duval?'

She flushed at the implication of his words. The insolence of the man, she thought, wishing she hadn't come.

'Shall we go?' she asked coldly. She marched past him.

They retraced their steps and walked up the staircase. He opened a door, and she stepped inside the first bathroom. Her heart sank as she recognised the cold, cavernous porcelain tub, the old-fashioned commode with its pull chain, the ugly cistern on the wall above it. Nothing had changed.

'You realise, of course,' he said, coming to stand beside her, 'that these bathrooms were modernised once at the turn of the century. Your husband is not maintaining them in their original purity, but in an outdated renovation.'

She looked up at him. 'Surely he knows that.'

He shrugged. 'I tried to tell him the other day. He wouldn't listen. Somehow he's got the idea I'm his enemy, that I'm looking for ways to oppose him. It's not true.'

Her eyes swept the room again, dismayed at the dingy sight. 'But, surely,' she began, then broke off, as it dawned on her that he was laughing beside her.

She gave him a sharp look, started to make a cutting remark, then found her own lips twitching until finally she was laughing with him.

She spread her hands. 'It's so—so—awful,' she said, trying to control herself.

He had such a nice smile, she thought. It changed his whole appearance. Suddenly, she was no longer afraid of him, no longer felt she disliked him.

'If you can convince him. . .' he began.

'No,' she interrupted sharply, fear returning to cloud her dark eyes. 'There's no chance of that.'

'All right,' he said quickly, and gave her another reassuring smile. 'We'll do it his way.' He took her lightly by the arm. 'Come on, I'll show you the rest of the upstairs while we're here.'

He conducted her through the other rooms, pointing out what had been done, what still needed to be done, asking her opinion on certain minor details.

By the time they had finished their tour of the upstairs and had come back down to the wide foyer, Lelia had forgotten her earlier antipathy towards the tall man entirely. He had answered her questions patiently, seemed genuinely interested in explaining the details of his work, and made her feel not only welcome, but as though her opinions mattered.

'Thank you for the tour, Mr Fielding,' she said. They were at the massive, carved double doors of the entrance now. 'It was very interesting—and instructive.'

'My pleasure.' He hesitated. 'Would you care for a cup of coffee before you go?'

She reacted automatically. 'Oh, no, I mustn't.'

The grave, kind expression on his face hardened imperceptibly. 'Another crucial appointment at the hairdresser's?' His tone was mocking.

Lelia flinched, hurt. 'No. It's not that.' She turned her head away. 'It's just that. . .'

'Sorry,' he broke in. 'That was a stupid remark. Will you forgive me?'

She gave him a shy glance and it seemed to her that he drew in his breath in a slight hissing sound. Then he smiled, the blue eyes softening.

'Just a quick cup,' he said. 'To plan our strategy. Maybe between us we can get your husband to change his mind about modernising the bathrooms.'

She was tempted, but it seemed vaguely disloyal to ally herself with this man against Armand, even in such an innocuous matter as that. She remembered his parting words that morning. Be careful. Was she about to make a terrible mistake?

Suddenly a brilliant shaft of sun broke in through the fanlight over the doorway. Outside in the mimosa tree by the house a mockingbird trilled its piercing song. The two workmen were sitting on the lawn under the tree eating their lunches from paper bags. A peaceful scene, she thought.

Lelia had a sudden, overpowering sense of freedom, of sheer pleasure just in being alive on such a beautiful day. It had been years, she thought, since she'd felt that way. Not since before her marriage.

'All right,' she said, and smiled up at him. 'One cup.'

CHAPTER THREE

HE HAD had taken over a portion of the servant's quarters to live in while he worked on the house. The job would take several weeks, perhaps months, to complete, and it was more convenient, he explained to her now, to live in the site.

'Don't you get lonely out here all by yourself?' she asked.

She was seated at the large work table by a window watching him as he made coffee on the hot plate. His movements were efficient, graceful, controlled, and he seemed totally at ease in the cluttered room.

'Lonely?' He cocked an eye at her as he measured coffee into a filter top. 'I'm too busy to get lonely. Besides,' he grinned, 'I get away occasionally.'

She glanced around the room. It had formerly been the communal room for the servants. There was a large native stone fireplace on one wall, a neatly made narrow bed in a corner, a chair, a lamp, a long counter where he had set up the hot plate along with a small refrigerator.

The table where she sat was littered with blue-prints and drawings. There was an empty coffee can full of sharp pencils, a slide rule, a notebook covered with figures. All very professional-looking, she thought, and although the room was cluttered, there was a pleasant, homey feeling to it.

'You must miss having a home of your own, though,' she said at last.

'Oh, I've had homes of my own. And I will again.'

He didn't elaborate. She wondered how many homes he'd had, how old he was. She looked at him. He stood easily beside the counter waiting for the coffee to drip. His hands were shoved into the back pockets of his jeans, his head bent, profile turned to her, and he whistled softly under his breath.

Middle thirties, she guessed. It was hard to tell with such a handsome man. Handsome? she thought, and looked at him more closely, comparing him with Armand who at one time had been her ideal of male beauty.

There was a dramatic difference between the two men, she thought. Armand was much younger, of course, softer, somehow, even before the accident. This man was hard, from the well-knit body and firm features to the decisive mind and strong will.

He carried the steaming mugs to the table and handed her one. 'Cream?' he asked. She nodded. Louisiana coffee, laced with chicory, was undrinkable by itself.

He went to the small fridge. 'I could make a sandwich,' he called over his shoulder. He turned and grinned. 'Nothing fancy.'

'No. No, thank you. Not today. Maybe next time.' Next time? she thought, surprised at her words. Why did I say that?

He sat down across from her at the table, pushed the papers aside and set down the cream, still in its carton.

'Your work must take you all over the world,' she said, pouring the cream into the thick black coffee. 'Armand tells me your services are very much in demand.'

He shrugged and reached for the carton of cream. 'It's not a very crowded field. Not everyone can tolerate the painstaking work.' He looked at her over his coffee cup, the blue eyes half-masked by long thick black eyelashes. 'Or the demanding customers.' He grinned to take the sting out of his words, and she couldn't help returning his smile.

'Are they all as bad as we are, then?' she asked lightly.

'It varies from country to country. Americans are far from the worst. The English don't trust foreigners. The French are tight-fisted with their francs. And so on.'

'Yet, you must like your work, to be so good at it, to stick to it.'

'I do. Very much. Every new house is a challenge. To stay as faithful as possible to the original architect's intentions, to modernise where possible without destroying the effect.'

She sighed. 'I envy you. I wish. . .' She broke off, knowing she was on the verge of disloyalty to Armand again.

He was staring at her now, and when she saw the look in those brilliant blue eyes, she regretted the moment of weakness that revealed too much. What was in the look?

Compassion? Yes, but something more, something far more disturbing than sympathy. She couldn't move. Something was passing between them that she couldn't define, but which made her heart begin to beat a little faster, her skin to feel a little warmer.

She remembered her original instinctive fear of this

man. The pleasant visit with him today, getting to know him better, had allayed that fear, and now she suspected that had been a mistake.

He was sitting perfectly still, never taking his eyes from her. Finally, she could bear the painful tension no longer. She took one last swallow of the cold coffee and rose to her feet.

'I must go,' she said. 'It's late.'

He got up then and set his cup down on the table. She was grateful to see that not with a word or a gesture did he try to keep her. In fact, she thought as he followed her across the room, he seems almost glad to see me go.

That night, at dinner, Lelia decided to tackle Armand on the subject of the bathrooms at Beaux Champs. She had spent the afternoon screwing up her courage, looking for the most prudent approach.

Luckily, Armand gave her the opening she was looking for himself. It was over dessert, a raspberry bombe he was especially fond of.

He wheeled his chair back a little from the table when he was finished and sighed with satisfaction. His long pale face seemed a little less pinched tonight under the glow of the chandelier, his expression not quite so irritable.

He looked at her. 'Well, Lelia, how did your little excursion go today?'

She heard Blanche's fork clatter to the table, saw the normally placid face suddenly contract with suspicion.

'What excursion?' she asked sharply.

Armand turned to her. 'Lelia is helping me at Beaux Champs. Protecting my interests against the terrible Mr

Fielding.' He laughed then, trivialising the whole thing. Blanche joined in nervously, and Tante Amalie fastened her beady eyes on her son in a sharply appraising look.

'Well, darling?' Armand drawled.

Lelia touched the linen napkin lightly to her lips and set it down on the table beside her plate. 'It was interesting,' she said calmly. It was now or never, she thought. She raised her eyes to meet Armand's. 'Did you know, Armand, that the bathrooms have already been remodelled once?' She made her voice casual. 'Mr Fielding said it was done around the turn of the century.'

Armand reached for his wine glass, his delicate tapering fingers curling around the fragile stem. He took one sip. 'Is that what he told you?'

A familiar droop of petulance began to form on the colourless lips. Lelia knew the signs, but plunged on. 'Yes. His view is that since they aren't in the original condition anyway, it wouldn't harm the effect to put in modern plumbing and fixtures.' She hesitated. 'Of course, he realises it's your decision. I made that quite clear.'

'Naturally it is Armand's decision,' Blanche put in heatedly. 'That man is far too arrogant and insurbodinate for his own good.' She turned to Armand. 'If he's going to turn your wife against you to get his own way, I think you should fire him.'

Lelia had to smile. She recalled quite clearly that Blanche had been one of the women in hot pursuit of the dashing Mr Fielding at the dance just two weeks ago.

'Mr Fielding could never turn me against Armand, Blanche,' she said quietly, 'and they both know it. It's Armand's decision, but'—here she turned back to her husband—'you did ask me to go, Armand, and I am only giving my opinion.' She shrugged. 'It doesn't really matter to me.'

Armand eyed her suspiciously over his wine glass. 'I'll think about it,' he said at last. He pushed his chair back farther. 'Shall we go into the drawing room?' he asked. 'And, Lelia, try tonight to pay attention to the game. It's no fun if I win too easily.'

She followed him, overjoyed at her success. She might not get the bathrooms she wanted at Beaux Champs, but she had said her piece and averted an argument. To her, that was a great victory.

Lelia didn't return to Beaux Champs for the next three weeks. She had decided that after the small point she had won, it would be prudent to stay away.

Finally, Armand asked her one day as he was leaving for the mill if she'd been, and she was glad to be able to reply truthfully.

'No,' she said. 'Did you want me to go again?'

They were in the long entrance hall, Lelia still in her dressing gown. At the door, he turned and looked up at her. 'That was our agreement, wasn't it? I want you to go today, if you have the time.' There was the hint of a sneer in his voice. 'I've decided to modernise the bathrooms after all, and I want you to make sure Fielding is following my instructions.' He handed her a piece of paper. 'This is a copy of the list I gave him.'

She took the paper from him and glanced at it, hoping her elation didn't show on her face. 'Very well, Armand. If you think it's necessary.'

When he was gone she flew into her bedroom to dress.

It was early April now, the most beautiful season in New Orleans, before the summer's oppressive heat and humidity descended.

She dressed in a simple skirt of rose-coloured polished cotton, a plain shirt of rose-and-white stripes. It was a balmy morning. She wouldn't even need a sweater.

As she drove the blue Thunderbird out of the French Quarter and down the River Road, her heart was light. At last she had something to look forward to. The giant dogwoods, mimosa and magnolias blazed on the banks of the Mississippi, a symphony in pink and white, and as she turned into the long curving drive of Beaux Champs, she could see the azaleas on either side just bursting into bloom.

There was a strange car parked in front of the house, a dusty station wagon with New York licence plates. She jumped out of the Thunderbird with a light step and walked briskly across the portico, feeling more alive than she had in years. The large double doors at the entance to the house were opened wide, and she stepped inside.

The two workmen in their white overalls were sanding the banister railing on the landing at the top of the stairs. One of them noticed her looking up at them and called down to her.

'Mornin', Miz Duval,' he said in a strong Cajun accent.

'Good morning,' she called back. 'I'm looking for Mr Fielding.'

'Back in his workroom, ma'am,' was the brief reply.

Lelia walked down the long hallway to the back of the house, through the kitchen to the servant's quarters. The door to his room was open, and she walked in.

He was standing at the work table by the window, a tall girl with long blonde hair that hung in a loose silky curtain to her shoulders beside him. Their backs were to Lelia, and they seemed deep in conversation. He had one hand resting lightly on the girl's shoulder, and with the other was pointing out something to her on the blueprint spread before them on the table.

They were both dressed in jeans. The girl had on a strapless knit top, and he was once again bare from the waist up.

Lelia stood at the doorway, her eyes fastened on that tanned muscular back, barely hearing the murmured conversation. Before she knew what was happening, she felt an intense surge of resentment rise up in her.

How dare he entertain his women friends in his employer's home, she thought angrily. She glanced over at the bed in the corner. It was made as neatly as it had been the last time she was here. That didn't prove anything.

Putting on her haughtiest manner, she rapped sharply on the open door. 'Excuse me,' she called out in a cold voice.

Both heads turned at once. The girl was quite beautiful, with a healthy rosy glow over her tanned face, wide-set eyes and strong features. Lelia felt more than ever like a hothouse flower, and her resentment deepened.

Then she saw the look on his face. His hand had dropped from the girl's shoulder as he turned, and the dazzling blue eyes were alight with pleasure. When he saw the lift of her chin and the expression on her face, however, the slow smile vanished and the eyes narrowed.

'My husband asked me to come out and check on the

bathrooms,' she said in an imperious tone, her voice cutting into the silence. 'I hope I'm not interrupting anything important.'

'Not at all, Mrs Duval,' he said easily. He turned to the girl. 'This is my assistant, Karen Swenson.'

Lelia nodded curtly at the girl, who murmured a brief greeting. The tall man came towards her now in long, easy strides until he stood before her. She *wished* he would put a shirt on. That smooth broad expanse of chest, the jeans hanging low on his narrow hips, the bare muscled arms, all unnerved her.

The blonde girl was his assistant, she thought, and the load of anger lightened slightly. Perhaps she was just helping him. Still, she knew that Armand wouldn't like it if he thought Mr Fielding had his mistress staying with him, even if she was a business associate.

'Would you like to go up now and take a look?' he asked easily. 'I have a few more instructions for Karen before she leaves.' His blue gaze was probing, as though he were trying to read her thoughts under the haughty mask. Then, in a lower tone, he added, 'She just stopped by on her way to another project in Houston.'

Lelia nodded. Why was he explaining this to her? She didn't care. Then why did she feel so relieved to hear that his relationship with the girl was business, that she hadn't spent the night with him?

She began to feel ashamed of her reaction, to question the sudden resentment at the sight of them standing there so close together at the table. Her head began to whirl in confusion.

'I'll just go on up, then,' she said, relieved to hear that her voice was steady. 'There's no need for you to come with me. We can discuss it later.'

She turned, then, and without a backward glance retraced her steps out into the foyer and up the stairs past the workmen. When she opened the door of the first bathroom, she was so overcome with delight that she could only stare in amazement at the transformation. Gone were the ugly porcelain tub, the cistern, the old-fashioned commode, and in their place were sparkling new cream-coloured modern fixtures. Yet, the wallpaper and wooden cabinets were in perfect accord with the period, softening the stark modern look, so that it conformed with the rest of the house even more than it had before.

She heard a step behind her and the firm deep voice.

'Well, what do you think?' he asked.

She whirled around, beaming with delight. 'Oh, Michael, it's perfect.'

He followed her inside, and for half an hour told her in meticulous detail exactly what he had done, explained his thinking and the mechanics involved as though he really did consider her a half-way intelligent woman instead of an incompetent doll.

'I know Armand will be pleased,' she said happily when they were through with the inspection and had started down the staircase.

She noticed that the workmen were gone. It must be their lunch time. She also noticed that Michael was still shirtless, and a little tremor of uneasiness began to nag at her. Michael, she thought. She had called him Michael. Should she have done that?

He was walking easily at her side, unconcerned, casual. 'How did you manage it?' he asked with a smile when they had reached the foyer. 'To convince your husband about the bathrooms?'

Without thinking, she replied, 'Oh, I just let him think it was his idea,' and felt immediately disloyal. She bit her lip.

'Women!' he exclaimed. 'So devious.'

He was grinning at her, and she had to smile back. After all, Armand would be as pleased as she was.

'Well, you men force us into it,' she replied lightly.

He threw back his head and laughed, then. The movement tightened the cords along the long column of his throat and the muscles of his chest and flat stomach rippled. As she watched him, the uneasiness began to return. She moved one step away from him towards the open door.

'I'd better be going, now,' she said, 'and let you get on with your work.'

'It's lunchtime. How about that sandwich?' When she hesitated, frowning, he added quickly, 'It won't be much. Just some cold ham and rye bread. I might be able to find a pickle or two if you like them.'

'I do,' she replied. 'Yes, I'd like that.'

'Good.'

While he made coffee and sandwiches at the counter in his work room, she sat at the table idly turning over the blueprints and drawings lying there. She glanced at him from time to time. He had put on another stained white shirt, and she felt much more at ease with him now.

He seemed totally absorbed in what he was doing. All his movements were effortless, and she wondered how such a large man could be so graceful. Even before the accident, Armand always moved in a stilted, awkward manner, and he was of much slighter build and height. Armand seemed to be constantly trying to maintain an aristocratic bearing, while this man had a natural, easy grace and confidence that didn't have to prove anything.

Once again, a little twinge of fear that she was being disloyal to her husband assailed her. She must stop comparing the two men. It wasn't fair. Poor Armand was bound forever to his wheelchair, and all his wealth and social position could not make up for what he had lost. He'd give it all up in a minute, she thought, to be able to walk, to live like a normal man again.

But would he? For the first time, she began to wonder about that. The accident had left him bitter, but there were times, she thought now, when he positively seemed to enjoy the power his helpless state gave him over the three women in his house, when he used their pity and concern to get his way, assert his authority.

'Well, it's not exactly dinner at Antoine's,' Michael said now, setting a plate down before her. He poured coffee and pulled up a chair next to her.

'It looks wonderful. We have a marvellous chef, but sometimes I get tired of gourmet fare. At the convent we always ate like this, good plain food.'

She took a bite of the thick ham sandwich and chewed appreciatively. He gave her a startled look.

'Don't tell me you were a nun!' he exclaimed. 'Although that would explain that cool, detached manner of yours. Every time I think you're finally beginning to relax and enjoy yourself, you pull back.'

She laughed. 'No, not a nun. My mother died when I was born, and my father wasn't able to keep me with

him—he was a mining engineer—so I was raised by the
Ursuline nuns down at Bayou Laforche.' She took a sip
of coffee. 'However, I married right out of the convent,
so that might explain my nunny habits.'

'You're distantly related to your husband, aren't you?'

'Yes. How did you know that?'

'Oh, Charles Donaldson mentioned it.'

Had he been questioning Charles about her? she
wondered. If so, what else had he told him?

'Charles and I play handball once a week,' he
explained casually, as if sensing her unease, 'and it
usually leads to a drink afterwards—or two.' He grinned,
hesitated, then added, 'Charles is very fond of you—and
your husband.'

It had started to rain, one of those unpredictable
spring cloudbursts that pour down relentlessly for a short
time then leave as suddenly as they come.

She looked out of the window. The sky, so blue and
sunny when she arrived at Beaux Champs that morning,
was a leaden grey, with a heavy bank of black clouds
moving in fast. The trees and shrubbery had taken on a
metallic bright green cast, and the rain fell in sheets
against the windowpane. She could hear deep rolls of
thunder in the distance.

She could feel his eyes on her and glanced nervously
across the table at him. He was sitting with his chair
tilted back, the coffee cup in his hand, legs apart, the
balls of his feet braced against the floor. The look on his
face was grave, but friendly. And also totally unnerving.

'Your assistant—Miss Swenson—is very beautiful,'
she said abruptly, just for something to say.

'Yes,' he agreed, 'she is.' He straightened his chair

then and rested his elbows on the table. 'It's Mrs Swenson, by the way, and in case your imagination ran away with you when you saw her here this morning, not only is she quite happily married, but I make it a firm practice to keep hands strictly off married women.' Lelia flushed and glanced down at her lap. She noticed that she was methodically ripping a paper napkin to shreds. The nuns would be horrified, she thought grimly, and made her hands still. He took a sip of coffee. 'Besides,' he added, 'she's not my type.'

'What is your type?' Lelia asked lightly, to cover her confusion. She hardly knew what she was saying.

He eyed her appraisingly. 'Oh, I've always been partial to dark women.' His eyes glinted mischievously. 'Especially pure Creole types, with creamy skin, black hair and the scent of magnolias. Right out of an *ante-bellum* novel. Something like you. You look as though you belong in a big crinoline skirt and a parasol.'

She flushed again. 'I'm not really like that at all,' she murmured. 'Besides, I'm married, too.' How did this conversation get started? she wondered. What is happening to me?

'I know that,' he said quietly. He grinned again. 'I allow myself to look and admire, even when I know I can't touch. Nothing wrong with that, is there?'

She didn't know how to answer that, and looked out of the window again, staring at the trees bending in the wind, the rain still coming down. As she watched, still at a loss for words, she noticed that the wind had shifted, causing a sudden lull in the storm.

Then, through the glass, she saw it. Not ten feet away, its frightened brown eyes staring wildly in confusion,

stood a little fawn. As she gazed into the terrified eyes of
the animal, Lelia was suddenly transported back five
years to her wedding day. Her food stuck in her throat,
and with a little cry she jumped up, overturning her chair
and upsetting her coffee.

No, she thought, in a panic, I can't bear it. She stood
there trembling, her hands over her eyes, as she relived
that dreadful day in her mind, the accident, its terrible
aftermath. She started sobbing uncontrollably, great
wracking sobs. Then she felt strong arms come around
her, pulling her up against a hard chest.

'Lelia, Lelia,' she heard him saying over and over
again. 'What is it?'

Her head was throbbing, her whole being pierced
through with the pain of memory. She looked up at him,
wild-eyed, almost out of control. 'The deer,' she choked
out. 'The deer.'

'It's all right,' he said soothingly. His hand was
stroking her hair, trying to comfort her. 'They come up
to the house occasionally looking for salt. Don't worry.
He'll find his way back to his mother. The storm won't
hurt him.'

He smiled reassuringly down at her, but she only
shuddered and buried her head in the hard shoulder.
'You don't understand,' she moaned.

'Tell me, then,' he said.

She pulled away and turned around. She felt she
couldn't bear to face him. He made no move to restrain
her or touch her. Finally, she began to collect herself,
and in a dull, low monotone, told him about the accident
that had crippled her husband.

He listened quietly, not uttering a word. When she

had finished, she felt drained, exhausted from the emotional upheaval, the effort of putting the dreadful story into words. But she also felt calmer and more at peace than she had for a long time.

'So you see,' she said in a muffled voice, her back still towards him, 'it's my fault, all my fault. I crippled Armand as surely as though I had pushed him off a cliff. I ruined his life.'

She felt strong gentle hands on her shoulders, then, and he turned her around to face him. She looked up at him, her eyes still glistening. He cupped her tear-stained face in the large hands and gazed down at her intently.

'Lelia, you reacted instinctively, not wilfully. How could that be your fault?' When she opened her mouth to protest, he put a finger on her lips. 'Shh,' he said, 'listen to me. You're a good Catholic. Surely you were taught that for an action to be sinful, there must be intent.'

That's what Father Pierre had told her. She nodded. 'I know that. I know that in God's eyes I'm innocent of actual sin, but to live with what I've done, day after day, year after year, to see him growing more bitter all the time. . .' She started to shiver, a cold chill passing through her. 'Sometimes I think he hates me. I know he does, and I can't blame him.'

'Oh, Lelia,' he said, drawing her to him again, his arms around her. 'What a hell he's put you through.'

She leaned against him, grateful for his strong, reassuring presence. Dimly she was aware that she shouldn't be standing here in his arms this way, but she felt almost giddy with relief that she had finally spoken of the tragedy locked inside her for so long, told someone about it who seemed to understand.

Gradually, the warmth of his body began to seep through to her. The shivering stopped, and in its place she felt a pleasant glow tingling through her, from the tips of her feet to the top of her head. The hand stroking her hair stopped, then slid slowly down to her back.

Her hands were on his shoulders, and she could feel the muscles tauten under the thin shirt, his quickened breath on the skin of her face. Instinctively, she clutched at him, and his arms tightened around her. He smelled of the outdoors, a clean masculine scent, mingled with a light, fresh aftershave. Looking up at him, she could see a little spot of fresh white paint on his temple, just beneath a lock of dark hair. His eyes were closed, the long thick lashes resting on the high prominent cheekbones.

He opened his eyes, then, the bright blue of them dazzling her, penetrating to her very soul. She sighed as the firm mouth came down and hungrily covered hers.

She had never been kissed like that before in her life, and it awakened in her an answering hunger that made her press more closely against him. Her lips parted, responding eagerly to his kiss, and her hands reached up into the unruly black hair.

Mindless now, forgetting even who she was, what she was, she felt only like a woman. His lips were soft and moist on her mouth, his hair crisp under her searching fingers, and everywhere his hand moved, on her back, her waist, her hips, it left a trail of fire.

Then, abruptly, she could sense his body tense against hers. His hands came to her shoulders, gripping them almost painfully. He moved a few inches away from her.

She opened her eyes. His head was turned so that all

she could see was his profile, the dark hair falling over his forehead. His jaw was set, his eyes shut. She thought she had never seen such a beautiful man and reached out a hand to run it along the high cheekbones, the flat planes, the strong jaw.

He looked at her then, and his hands dropped from her shoulders. In that instant, she suddenly came to her senses, realised what she had done. With a little cry, she raised a fist to her mouth and bit hard at the knuckles.

'Lelia,' he said. 'I'm so sorry. Please forgive me.'

Forgive him? How could she blame him? With one stricken look, she turned and stumbled out of the room. She ran down the long hallway, past the stairs to the foyer.

She heard him coming after her, calling to her. 'Lelia. Wait.'

At the door, she felt his grip on her arm, forcing her around to face him. She couldn't look at him. He thrust something into her hands. She looked down. It was her handbag, left behind on the table in her mad dash from the room.

'Lelia, listen to me. Please listen to me.'

'I. . .I. . .' She couldn't speak. She just stood there clutching her bag in her hands, wanting to die.

'Nothing happened, Lelia,' she heard him say in a low earnest tone. 'Nothing at all. You were upset. You needed a shoulder to cry on. I just happened to be there. It could have been Charles. It could have been anybody.' He hesitated. 'Lelia, look at me. Please look at me.'

Finally, she raised her eyes. His hand left her arm, and he sighed. 'That's better.' His face was grave. He took a deep breath, then smiled. 'I haven't forgotten what I said about not touching married women. It's just that you don't seem married to me. You seem so untouched.' The smile vanished. 'Perhaps you are, at that.' He looked away. 'Have you ever considered leaving him? Making a real life for yourself?'

She shook her head vigorously. 'Oh, no,' she said emphatically, finding her voice at last. 'I can never do that.'

'No,' he said, his eyes on her once again, 'I don't suppose you could.' He was silent for a moment, then said, 'The job here is almost completed. I'll be moving on. If I don't see you before I go, I want you to promise me one thing.' His voice took on a harsh note. 'Promise me you'll give up this martyr role your husband has cast you in. I can see why you feel you must stay married to him, but for God's sake, Lelia, quit letting him feed off you. He's like a vampire, sucking your life's blood.'

She looked away. 'You don't understand,' she mumbled.

'Oh, yes, I do. I understand quite well. I'm a man, too. I know the temptation all men feel when they're confronted with a woman like you. You almost beg to be dominated, with that remote beauty, that chaste look that doesn't quite hide the fire burning underneath.'

She reddened, remembering her abandonment to his kiss, and gave him a quick look. 'That's not fair.'

He shrugged. 'Life isn't fair. But it's still what we make it.' He sighed and ran a hand through his dark hair. 'I don't know. Maybe it's too late for you. I only know it was a vital, passionate woman I kissed back there, and not a china doll.' The blue, blue eyes bored into her, and her gaze faltered.

'I must go,' she said. She quickly turned and ran

outside to the car. She couldn't bear to hear any more. He was wrong about her, wrong about Armand. He had to be.

CHAPTER FOUR

IN ANOTHER month, the work on Beaux Champs was completed. After her last visit and the upsetting emotional encounter with Michael, Lelia had assiduously avoided the place, pleading a headache or lack of interest whenever Armand asked her to go out there alone.

She had given in and gone with him twice, but made certain each time that she and the tall, disturbing man were never alone together. He had said that day of the storm that nothing had happened, and she made up her mind to believe him. There was nothing in his manner towards her when they met to change it.

Her life resumed its old secure, futile pattern. Armand invited Michael to dinner twice in the month after her last visit to Beaux Champs alone. Once he had refused. The second time, he accepted, but when they met his manner was as polite and distant as her own.

Now he would be leaving, and she was torn between relief that she would no longer have to avoid his disturbing presence and regret for what might have been. She knew, however, where her duty lay. There was no question in her mind, and in the rare moments of weakness when she lay alone in her ornate canopied bed at night and allowed herself to feel again that one kiss burning on her mouth, she struggled hard against the feverish weakness that stole through her body, vowing to try even harder to please Armand, to make him happy.

It was growing warmer and more humid each day in New Orleans. The bright red bougainvillea that twined around the wrought-iron trellis in the courtyard at the back of the house on Chartres Street was beginning to show colour. Soon the deep pink crape myrtle would be in bloom, and the roses.

Lelia had finally persuaded Armand to allow her at least to do some volunteer charity work, and this filled her days to some extent, made her feel of some use in the world.

On one exceptionally warm, brilliant day in late May, she was returning to the house from a charity luncheon at the Hotel Monteleone, not five blocks away in the heart of the French Quarter. She had walked the short distance. The streets were jammed now with tourists, and she was glad to get home, out of the glare of the sun, the jostling of the crowds thronging the pavements and into the cool, quiet dimness of the house.

With a sigh of relief, she shut the heavy carved door behind her and started across the tiled floor of the foyer to her bedroom. She wanted a bath badly. Her new sleeveless linen dress was clinging to her limply and little beads of perspiration dampened her forehead.

As she passed by the drawing room, she heard Armand's voice call out to her. 'Lelia. Is that you?'

'Yes, Armand.' She walked inside and stopped short just inside the doorway.

There, standing at the window, his back towards her, was Michael. He turned, and for a brief moment the blue eyes held hers. He was dressed in a pair of light grey trousers that moulded his slim hips and long legs, a discreetly checked blue-and-white shirt and a navy blue linen blazer. Taken unawares, Lelia caught her breath at the sight of him. The crisp black hair had been recently cut, he was clean-shaven, and looked more breathtakingly handsome even than she had remembered him.

'Good afternoon, Mrs Duval,' he said politely, then glanced away.

Collecting herself from the first stunning impact of his presence, she murmured a greeting, then deliberately crossed the room to Armand's side. She leaned down and kissed him lightly on his pale cheek.

'Well, my dear, have you been out rescuing widows and orphans? Or is it prison inmates today?' His gaze shifted to the tall man at the window. 'My wife has become a doer of good works.'

'Very commendable,' Michael said shortly.

Then she noticed that Charles Donaldson was in the room. He had been sitting behind Armand, half-hidden by the wide curves of a tapestried wing chair. He stood up now to greet her.

'How have you been, Lelia? You're looking as lovely as ever.'

She smiled then. She liked Charles, felt at ease with him, and knew that Armand trusted him with his wife, as well as the family's legal business.

'Quite well, Charles,' she replied. 'A little the worse for the heat and crowds out there at the moment.'

'Well, gentlemen,' Armand interjected briskly, 'I guess that takes care of our business.' He looked up at Lelia. 'Mr Fielding has come to say goodbye. His work is finished. Charles and I went out to inspect Beaux Champs this morning, and I must say I am quite satisfied.'

Then, suddenly, the brown eyes narrowed at her. A frown crossed the pinched features and the thin mouth drooped. Lelia froze. She knew that look. What had she done? She clutched nervously at her handbag.

'What in the world is that you're wearing, Lelia?' came the high-pitched voice.

She glanced down at the pale yellow dress. It was one she had chosen for herself recently off the rack at one of the large department stores on Canal Street. She had bought it on an impulse one day because she liked the style. It was less close-fitting, more casual than what she usually wore, and she felt more comfortable in it than the high-fashion clothes Armand chose for her.

'It's just a dress, Armand,' she said lightly.

'You know I don't like you in yellow, Lelia. It washes out your complexion.'

'It's a very pale yellow, Armand.' She smiled, trying to make a joke of it.

The cold expression on her husband's face was unyielding. His bloodless lips curled in a sneer, and he sighed elaborately.

'You see what happens, Lelia, when you insist on choosing for yourself.' He looked her up and down. 'The neckline is all wrong for you, and the style. . .' He shook his head. 'It makes you look more than ever fresh out of the convent.' Then his voice hardened. 'Go change. Now.'

'Armand,' she began. Why was he doing this to her, humiliating her in front of the other two men? She couldn't believe his spiteful attitude was only over a dress. What should she do? She would either have to obey him or defy him and create a scene. She heard

Charles clear his throat, then there was dead silence in the room.

As she stood there debating what to do, with Armand's taunting gaze still on her, waiting for her to obey him, Michael Fielding's deep voice cut into the stillness.

'I thought it was a woman's prerogative to choose her own clothes.' His tone was mild, but with an underlying hardness that made Lelia glance over at him in surprise.

When she met the blue gaze, she saw a fleeting smile cross his face and there was a slight shrug to the broad shoulders. Quickly, she looked back at Armand. Somehow, Michael's comment and the brief shared look gave her the courage she needed.

'Let's discuss it later, shall we, Armand?' she said in a pleasant tone.

She turned to Charles, but not before she had seen the swift look of malevolence cross her husband's face. I'll pay for this later, she thought, and made up her mind to be especially nice to him tonight.

'How have you been, Charles?' she asked, crossing over to his side. 'We haven't seen much of you lately.'

Then, from behind her, she heard Armand's voice. 'You'll be anxious to get going, I'm sure, Mr Fielding. I won't keep you. I believe our business is concluded.'

She turned, saw Michael nod his head, then walk towards her and Charles. When he reached them, he held out a hand to Charles.

'Goodbye, Michael,' Charles said warmly. 'I've enjoyed our handball games in spite of never winning. Where do you go from here?'

'I have a job to finish up out in Houston, then I go on to Philadelphia for a few months. After that, I'm not sure.'

Charles laughed. 'You are a rolling stone. Well, I hope you get back down to New Orleans one day. I'd like to even that lopsided score.' He turned to Lelia. 'This man's a demon on a handball court. I've never seen anyone so big move so fast.'

Lelia could well imagine that, recalling the muscular strength of his body, the lithe grace of his movements. He turned to her then and held out a hand.

'Goodbye, Mrs Duval. It's been a pleasure working with you. Perhaps we'll meet again.'

She took his hand. 'Perhaps,' she murmured, and gave him a cool, remote smile.

His hand was warm, and as he pressed hers lightly, she realised how much she hated to see him go. Even though she had avoided him, it had been an odd comfort just to know he was close by.

He dropped her hand, then, and without another word or a backward glance, walked out of the room. He didn't shake hands with Armand, she noticed, or say goodbye to him. She heard the front door open and close, and then he was gone.

She glanced at Armand. He was staring at the doorway of the room, a brooding, thoughtful expression on his face. Lelia sighed and turned to Charles.

'Would you like a drink?' She called to her husband. 'Armand?'

'No,' he said shortly. 'I don't feel well. I think I'll go and lie down.'

Before she could offer to help him, he had wheeled out of the room, leaving behind a tense silence. Finally, Charles spoke.

'I think I'll have that drink. Join me?'

'All right.' She crossed over to the drinks cabinet beside the marble fireplace and took down two glasses and a bottle of wine. 'Sherry?' she called to him.

'Yes. That's fine.'

He came to stand beside her and watched her as she poured the wine. She tried to keep her fingers from trembling, but a reaction to the ugly scene with Armand over the dress had set in. She dreaded what she knew was ahead of her. Somehow Armand would find a way to punish her for her open defiance.

'Lelia,' Charles began in a low voice, 'I know it's none of my business, but. . .'

'Don't, Charles. Please don't.' She turned to face him and forced a smile at the look of concern on his kind face.

He held up a hand. 'Let me finish.' He took a sip of wine, then heaved a deep sigh. 'How much do you know about Armand's business affairs?'

She gave him a startled look. 'Very little. He gives me everything I need. I hardly handle any money at all. Why do you ask?'

Charles drained his glass and set it down on the cabinet. 'The Duval family's financial situation is a peculiar one, and I think there are some aspects of it you should know about.'

He poured himself another glass of wine, walked over to the window and drew aside the heavy damask drapery. He stood there staring outside for a moment.

'Aside from the textile mill and the sugar plantation, there is also a family corporation, with Armand and Amalie the sole shareholders. Virtually all the Duval money is tied up in these corporations, and the articles and by-laws of each entity clearly state that all shares and all liquid assets—meaning money—remain in the corporation. Nothing passes to Armand's wife.'

Lelia was bewildered. 'But what does that mean to me, Charles? I don't understand why you're telling me this.'

Charles turned around and gave her a long look. 'I'm telling you that there is virtually no community property. If you were to divorce Armand, you would hardly get a penny. You could sue the family corporation, but I doubt if you'd win, especially with Armand's helpless physical condition.'

Lelia could only stare at him. 'But, Charles, I have no intention of leaving Armand. How could you think such a thing?'

He crossed swiftly to her side, then, and gazed down at her with a determined, serious look.

'How could I not think such a thing?' he ground out. 'I've stood by for five years now and watched him trying to destroy you, using you, punishing you, feeding off you to satisfy his own perverted self-pity.'

Shocked, Lelia put a hand to her throat. 'Charles, you don't understand. I was the cause of the accident. You know that. I could never hurt Armand in any way, ever again. I owe him my life. If it weren't for me. . .'

'You owe him nothing,' Charles broke in, his voice low and insistent. 'Lots of men have handicaps, and rise above them. If Armand chooses to wallow in self-pity, that's his privilege, but I can't just stand by and watch him destroy you in the process.'

Lelia lowered her eyes. She knew there was some truth in what he said, but he wasn't the one who had to live with the grinding sense of guilt. Besides, even though Armand was occasionally cruel to her, enjoyed the exercise of his authority over her, still he was good to her in many ways. And he needed her. Even if it was only to satisfy a perverted self-pity, as Charles had pointed out.

'Please, Charles,' she murmured, 'I don't want to talk about it any more, not ever again.' She turned from him. 'I think you'd better go.'

He was silent for a while, then said, 'All right. I had to try. I just want you to know that if you ever do decide to escape from this prison he's put you in, I'll be there, waiting. I. . .'

He broke off then, set his glass down and left.

As she dressed for dinner that night, Lelia thought over what Charles had said that afternoon. Michael had said virtually the same thing that day out at Beaux Champs when she'd told him about the accident and her crippling sense of guilt. So had old Father Pierre when she'd gone to him to confess her crime.

Could they be right? She looked at her reflection in the mirror, at the hated artificial coiffure and silk designer dress that made her look like a parody of her real self. Her real self? Did she even have a self any more?

She put her hands over her face and shuddered a long sigh. Perhaps she had paid enough for what she had done. No amount of penance would make Armand walk again or rekindle the love she once thought she had for him. Was it all a waste?

She looked into the mirror again. I can never leave Armand, she thought, but perhaps it's possible that I can make more of a life for myself, be who I am, even find out who I am, instead of merely existing like this as a pampered household pet.

A tiny spark of hope began to kindle in her heart. She liked her new charity work, but raising money at luncheons and balls was not enough. She wanted to become more directly involved with the retarded children, the delinquent girls, the abandoned mothers.

I'll cut my hair, she thought daringly, dress to please myself. For the first time in years, she began to know what it was like to feel alive, like a human being with work she could do, a function in the world that perhaps she alone could fulfil.

I'll speak to Armand, she thought as she walked down the hall to go in to dinner. And if he refuses? She lifted her chin. Then I'll have to find a way.

The others were all seated at the long dining table, gleaming under the chandelier with snowy white damask, crystal goblets, silverware and china. Armand gave her a quick glance as she took her place. She thought he looked paler tonight than usual, and wondered just how angry he was at her defiance of him that afternoon over the dress.

'You're late,' he said in an accusing tone.

'I'm sorry, Armand,' she said calmly, and for once her heart didn't jump wildly at his reprimand. 'You could have started without me.'

As they ate, Lelia listened idly to their conversation, wondering if it would be better to broach the subject of enlarging the scope of her charitable activities now or wait until she and Armand were alone. Or, perhaps, she thought, say nothing and just do it.

They were discussing the completion of the restoration at Beaux Champs.

'It would be nice to move out there for the summer,' Tante Amalie was saying. 'Before the hot weather. Then we would be all settled by the time the fall season began.'

'Yes, but I think we should have a large reception right away,' Blanche put in excitedly. 'Invite all our friends to show off the place.'

Lelia knew they wouldn't expect or ask for her opinion, and continued eating in silence, listening, thinking.

'I haven't decided yet,' Armand said. 'I've been thinking it might be better to wait until fall to move. There are a few more details still to be finished up.'

Blanche snorted daintily. 'I thought that man—Fielding—had finished his job and been paid off.'

'Oh, yes,' Armand drawled. 'He's gone.'

Lelia felt his eyes on her, but said nothing.

'Thank goodness for that,' Blanche commented with some vehemence. 'What an insolent man. I don't see how you put up with him, Armand.'

'He did his job,' Armand replied mildly. 'Lelia helped see to that, didn't you, darling?'

Before she could think of an answer to that enigmatic statement, Blanche interrupted. 'Lelia!' There was a genuine note of scorn underlying her teasing tone. 'It seems all she did was conspire with the man against your wishes.'

Armand frowned at that, and Lelia watched as Blanche's triumphant expression faltered in the face of his disapproval. She seemed confused, not so sure now how to proceed. Armand darted a glance at Lelia.

'Did you do that, Lelia?' he asked lazily, leaning back in his chair.

Lelia met his gaze. 'I hope not, Armand,' she replied calmly. 'I certainly never had any intention of doing so.'

Blanche laughed. 'Well, of course, some women around here did seem to find him irresistible.'

Including you, Lelia thought, and suddenly she had had enough of this baiting. Why should she have to put up with it? It was only out of habit that she did so. Blanche had no power or authority over her. Surely pleasing Armand didn't extend to suffering Blanche's taunting insults in silence?

She set her fork down carefully on her plate and turned to Blanche, staring directly into her eyes. 'Are you insinuating, Blanche, that I either sought or engaged in an affair with Michael Fielding?' She saw the pale blue eyes widen in disbelief at the stark question. 'Because if you are, I think you owe me—and Armand—an apology.'

There was total silence in the room. Only Tante Amalie, her beady black eyes missing nothing, continued to eat.

'Well, Blanche?' Armand said at last. 'What do you have to say to that?'

'Well, of course,' Blanche faltered, 'I was implying no such thing, and of course I apologise to you both if Lelia considers I insulted her.' She hesitated, then murmured, 'However, I don't recall saying anything at all remotely suggesting an affair. That was all Lelia's idea, Armand, you'll have to admit.'

Lelia felt all three pairs of eyes on her now, and

something in her stomach plunged sickeningly. Why had she said that? Blanche had only been baiting her to make her look poor to Armand, to try to enhance her own position.

She couldn't read the look on Armand's face. It was an inscrutable mask. Surely he didn't believe she would do such a thing. But instinctively she knew that to deny it, to defend herself further against Blanche's insidious innuendoes, would only worsen the situation.

Finally, Armand pushed his chair back from the table. 'Shall we go into the drawing room?' he said calmly.

She waited for him that night in her bedroom, knowing he would come to her. She dreaded the scene she knew was in store for her, both for her defiance of him over the dress that afternoon and the conversation at dinner. In a way she would be glad to get it over with. Anything was better than that sullen silence.

She had wondered for some time, from the very beginning, why he had insisted on throwing her and Michael Fielding together. Now she was almost certain that he had been testing her, tempting her to see how far her loyalty and fidelity to him went. It was a disgusting thing to do, she thought, especially when she tried so hard to please him.

He had hardly spoken to her over the chess game, and she had played so badly that he gave up early in disgust. She had pleaded a headache, then, and gone to her room.

After her bath, she had covered her flimsy nightgown with the heavy white velvet robe and got into bed with a book. She couldn't concentrate, and when the knock finally came, she put the book aside with relief and some apprehension.

'Come in,' she called.

But it was Peter whose head appeared at the door, and not Armand.

'Excuse me, madam,' he said. He was not in his chauffeur's uniform, but in the nondescript black suit he wore inside the house when he tended to Armand's needs.

'What is it, Peter?'

'It's Mr Duval, madam.' There was a note of subdued panic in his voice. 'He's had a fall and I can't seem to rouse him.'

Lelia jumped out of bed and ran down the hall to Armand's bedroom. She saw him lying on the bed, dressed in his red brocade dressing gown, his eyes closed, his body still.

Peter was behind her, peering anxiously over her shoulder.

'What happened, Peter?' She reached down to take the limp wrist in her hand.

'He was getting into bed,' Peter explained in a halting, apologetic voice. 'He always gets into bed by himself. I was in the bathroom, hanging up his towels and getting his medicine.'

'Yes? Then what happened?' His pulse was weak and slow, but definitely there. As she stared down at him, her heart in her mouth, she thought she saw the waxen eyelids flutter.

'I heard a noise. Then he cried out, and I came back. He was lying on the floor. He must have slipped. I picked him up and put him on the bed and when I couldn't rouse him, I went to get you immediately.'

Lelia's mind raced. He could have bumped his head, she thought, but there was no object near the bed that he could have hit with enough force to knock him out. What she was really afraid of, she realised, was his heart.

Then she made up her mind. She couldn't risk waiting for him to regain consciousness. If it was his heart, he'd need immediate medical attention. She turned to Peter.

'Call an ambulance,' she said briskly, 'then stay with him while I get dressed.'

During the next week, Charles was like a rock to Lelia. Blanche and Tante Amalie, for all their efficient airs and authoritative dominance of the household, were useless. Hysterical at first, when Lelia woke them that night to tell them she was going to the hospital with Armand, then later dissolving in helpless tears, they left the whole burden to fall on Lelia's shoulders.

He never regained consciousness. The heart condition that had plagued him since childhood finally took its toll, and he died peacefully, without suffering.

Charles was with her in the waiting room at the hospital when the doctor came to tell her, and although she had been expecting the worst, it still came as a shock to her to know he was really gone.

After that, an indescribable numbness settled over her. With Charles's help, she went through all the necessary motions, made the funeral arrangements, sent out the old-fashioned black-edged announcements to their friends, and somehow got through the next week.

Tante Amalie and Blanche lay prostrate in their rooms until the day of the funeral, of no help at all to Lelia in making decisions. When she asked their opinion, they only waved her away, lost in their grief.

It wasn't until the day of the funeral that Lelia allowed herself to examine her own sorrow. It was then, during the funeral mass at the Basilica in Jackson Square where they had been married, with all of New Orleans society in attendance, that it really sank into her that Armand was dead. As she knelt there, praying for his immortal soul, the five painful years of their marriage vanished from her mind, and she thought of him only as she had known him and cared for him before the accident. Tears of love and pity stung her eyes and ran down her cheeks under the heavy black veil.

That was the real Armand, she thought as the mourners filed out of the church and into the waiting black limousines. He had been so charming, then, with his blond good looks, the pale face and delicate aristocratic, patrician features.

He was buried in the Old Cemetery on Rampart Street where the Duval family had had a crypt for generations. Because New Orleans was below sea level, burials all had to be made above ground, and as Lelia watched the black-clad pallbearers insert the narrow casket into the tall tomb, she was glad that he would not be buried in the ground.

She glanced around, dry-eyed now, at the large group of mourners. Charles was at her side, his hand on her arm a solid comfort and support. Blanche and Tante Amalie were sobbing noisily. Peter was there. He seemed to be genuinely sorry at the death of his master.

The priest chanted the last prayer, and the door of the crypt clanged shut. Lelia shuddered at the finality of the sound. She still had one last ordeal to get through. The Duval family's position in society demanded that she provide food and drink at the house on Chartres Street so that Armand's friends could pay their last respects to his widow. Then it would be over.

She turned to go, and as she walked out of the cemetery towards the waiting limousine, Charles at her side, she thought she saw out of the corner of her eye a familiar tall figure with black hair standing at the back of the crowd.

Then she was inside the car, the incident forgotten. She must have been mistaken. Why would Michael Fielding come all this way to the funeral of a man he didn't even like?

Charles remained at the house after all the guests had gone. The other two women had gone upstairs to their own quarters, and he and Lelia were alone in the drawing room. Peter had unobtrusively cleared away the worst of the aftermath of the guests, and the room seemed suddenly very still and quiet. She felt so tired, she thought, drained emotionally and physically. She sat down wearily on the brocaded couch; put her head back and closed her eyes. Then she heard Charles come to sit beside her.

'Here,' he said. She opened her eyes, and he thrust a wineglass into her hand. 'You could use this.'

She thanked him with a smile, took a sip and leaned her head back again with a long sigh.

Charles cleared his throat. 'This may not be the time, Lelia, to bring up business affairs, but I'm going to enter the will for probate Monday, and I think you should know where matters stand so you can make plans.'

She opened her eyes. 'You already explained, Charles. I understand. I'm to have nothing.' She saw him frown and put a hand on his arm. 'It's all right. It's time I made some use of my life, anyway.'

He smiled then. 'It's not quite that bad. As I told you before, the bulk of the estate remains tied up in the family corporation. Or course, you own your own clothes, jewels, and the Thunderbird was a gift, in your name. There's also a small legacy from Armand's personal estate, enough to carry you for a year or so.' He hesitated. 'I'm sure that Amalie will give you a home, a comfortable one, for the rest of your life. Or until you marry again.'

'Yes, she said slowly, 'I'm sure she would. I've thought about that.' She looked at him. 'I decided it wasn't what I wanted. I'll never marry again, and I'd really and truly rather be on my own. I can work.'

'Well, in that case,' Charles went on, with something like relief in his voice, 'I should tell you that Armand did own this house outright and has left it to you. Beaux Champs stays in the family, but this house is yours to do with as you like.'

She thought this over. 'Whatever I like?'

He nodded. 'You can live in it—although it will be more than you can afford to keep it up—or sell it. It's yours absolutely. I'm sure Amalie and Blanche will move back to Beaux Champs as soon as possible anyway now that the restoration is completed. You'll be free to live any way you choose.'

Free, she thought, hardly daring to believe it. What would she do with her freedom? And what would be its price? She stared down into the amber wine in the delicate crystal goblet. Perhaps, she thought, I've already paid part of it.

CHAPTER FIVE

As LELIA had anticipated, Tante Amalie and Blanche were aghast when she told them her plans. She had thought it over very carefully, however, and knew what she wanted to do, what she had to do.

She found the opportunity at dinner one night, three weeks after Armand's funeral. The other two women had been discussing the move back to Beaux Champs, and Tante Amalie had just asked Lelia when she could be ready to go, when she dropped her bombshell.

'I'm not going back to Beaux Champs with you, Tante,' she said. Her heart was pounding, but she made her voice outwardly calm. 'I've decided to stay on here.'

'You can't possibly mean it, Lelia.' Tante Amalie's little black eyes bored into her, and Blanche's fork clattered on to her plate. 'Your place is with us, with the family. And, besides, you can't afford to stay here on your own.'

'No,' Lelia replied, 'I can't. I've decided to rent out the upstairs apartment.'

Blanche finally found her voice. 'Rent out the upstairs apartment!' she cried. '*Our* apartment?'

'You and Tante Amalie won't be exactly homeless,' Lelia responded drily. 'You have Beaux Champs—and enough money to buy ten town-houses if you choose.'

'It's out of the question,' Tante Amalie said firmly, and calmly continued eating her dinner. 'We will move out to the plantation next week.' She fixed Lelia with a determined stare. 'All three of us. The plans are all made.'

Her firm tone roused a habitual feeling of anxiety in Lelia, and she wavered. How could she defy this woman she had obeyed for so long, the woman who had taken her in when she had nowhere else to go? Then she thought of the endless rounds of social activity, the boring empty days of her past life, and her resolution strengthened.

'Whose plans, Tante?' she asked slowly. 'Yours? Blanche's? I'm very grateful for all you've done for me, but I must have a life of my own, a home of my own. Don't you see?'

'No, I don't see.' Tante Amalie laid her knife and fork down carefully on the fine china plate. 'How can you manage on your own? You're virtually penniless, entirely dependent on Duval money for your very subsistence.'

Lelia lifted her chin. 'There's a little money, enough to see me through for quite a while. I own the house. And I can work.'

Blanche snorted. 'And just what can you do that anyone would pay you for? Model expensive clothes? You've never done a day's work in your life.'

Lelia hadn't quite worked that out yet, but she was able-bodied, had been given a good basic education by the nuns, and was willing to try almost anything. She was certain she'd be able to find work.

'Then it's about time I did,' she said. 'I'll find something. I can type. Give music lessons. Work in a shop.' She spread her hands. 'How do I know what I can do until I try?'

'And what about us?' Blanche's voice rose dramatically. 'Have you thought what it will do to our position if you hire yourself out as a clerk in a store or type in an office? A Duval?'

'There's nothing to be ashamed of in honest work,' Lelia replied hotly. 'I'll take my maiden name back if that's what's worrying you.'

She and Blanche glared at each other across the table now. I will not back down, Lelia promised herself. If I give in now I'll be lost. The opportunity to escape will never come again, or the will to take it.

Then Tante Amalie's calm authoritative voice broke the hostile silence. 'Very well, Lelia. I can see that you refuse to consider our position, what your insane plan will do to Blanche and me. But what about Armand?'

Lelia's eyes flew to meet the tiny black buttons. 'Armand? What does he have to do with it? Armand is dead.'

'My son worshipped you,' the old woman went on. 'He gave you everything. Your every whim was satisfied. Now you tell me you intend to betray his memory, his love, his trust, by a course of action you know he would detest.'

Lelia felt the bitter tears sting her eyes. 'That's not fair, Tante,' she choked out. She lowered her head and stared miserably at her plate. 'If Armand loved me, he would want me to be happy.'

Tante Amalie's voice cut into the room like a knife. 'It was Armand's love for you that crippled him!' She rose from her chair and glared down at Lelia.

The old familiar load of guilt threatened once more to engulf her. Was it true? Certainly her one thoughtless action had caused the accident, but Armand had chosen himself to cripple his mind, his emotions.

She thought of Charles, Father Pierre, Michael Fielding—all had tried to convince her that she was not morally responsible for Armand's condition, for what he had made of it. She had been a good wife, done everything in her power to please him, even at the cost of her own self-esteem.

She raised her eyes then. 'My mind is made up, Tante,' she said quietly, and quailed inwardly at the look of hatred and contempt on the old woman's face.

'Very well, Lelia. Then there's nothing more to say.' She paused, then went on. 'Except that your defiance of my wishes, your husband's wishes, marks the end of our relationship. You will live to bitterly regret what you've done. For my part, I wash my hands of you.' She turned to Blanche. 'Come, Blanche. We must start packing. Lelia will want us out of her house as soon as possible.'

A week later they were gone, taking with them boxes of china, crystal, silver, and even most of the furniture in the upstairs apartment. A large moving van had simply appeared one morning, and two white-uniformed men had begun packing things from the kitchen and carrying furniture out.

As she watched them, Lelia thought that most of what they were taking probably belonged by rights to her under the terms of Armand's will. There were priceless antiques and whole sets of old porcelain and glassware. She didn't want it. She didn't even like most of it. If it would make them happy, let them have it.

When they were finally gone, taking the Rolls and an apologetic Peter with them, Lelia wandered through the house to take stock of what was left to her. They hadn't touched the ground floor, and there was enough there to furnish the now practically bare upstairs apartment quite adequately.

She knew she wouldn't have any trouble renting it out. Such large, airy apartments in the French Quarter were rare and commanded high rents.

Charles had helped her dispose of all Armand's belongings, so that his room was bare. Still, the task before her was almost insurmountable. She'd just have to get used to making decisions and arranging her own business affairs. It would take time, but there was no hurry.

The first thing she did after the two women left was to walk up to a large department store on Canal Street to buy some new clothes. She had already transferred most of her old expensive designer outfits into the empty closet in Armand's room, keeping only a few things she thought would be suitable for her new life.

She bought two pairs of blue jeans, some plainer underwear than the handmade silk lingerie she was used to, cotton shirts and a pair of tennis shoes. She had opened a bank account in her name to deposit the money advanced to her from Armand's estate, and paid cash for all her purchases for the first time in her life.

She had to smile at the looks she got from the salesgirls. They must wonder, she thought, what this society woman in the Givenchy suit and expensive air was doing buying such cheap plain clothes.

When she got back to the house on Chartres Street, she took her purchases into her bedroom and stood at the dressing table for a moment gazing at her reflection in the mirror. It was the same old Lelia, she thought, but with a subtle difference. There was a little more colour in the creamy complexion, a new sparkle in the dark eyes.

She took off the jacket of her suit and set to work, putting away her new clothes and clearing most of the expensive cosmetics and perfumes off the top of the dressing table. One thing led to another, and soon she was cleaning out drawers.

I'd better change my clothes, she thought, glancing down at the dishevelled silk blouse. Even though she didn't plan to wear many of her old couturier fashions any more, she didn't want to ruin them.

A stray lock of hair had come loose from the elaborate chignon at the top of her head. She tried to tuck it back in several times, but it wouldn't stay. Finally, in exasperation, she gave up. It's time I had it cut, anyway, she decided, and made up her mind to do so that very afternoon.

First, though, she'd get something to eat. She went down the hall to the kitchen. It was a large light room, with a round oak table in one corner by a window where Peter and the cook had eaten their meals. The refrigerator and cupboards were well-stocked with canned and frozen food, and she could use the servants' crockery and utensils.

She had taken out bread and cheese and was about to make some coffee when the front doorbell rang. Perhaps a prospective tenant, she thought. She'd placed an ad in the *Times-Picayune* which had appeared for the first time that morning. She wiped her hands on a towel and ran down the hall to the foyer.

When she opened the door and saw Michael Fielding

standing there, she drew back, startled. He had on a white dress shirt, open at the neck, dark trousers, and a light greyish-blue jacket. Her first reaction on seeing him at her door was one of pleasure. Just looking at him gave her spirits a lift. Then, quickly, she resumed her old remote mask.

'Mr Fielding,' she said quietly. 'I had no idea you were in New Orleans.' She wondered why he was staring at her so intently.

'I'm just passing through on my way to Houston,' he said at last, 'and thought I'd stop by to see how you were getting along. And to offer my condolences on the death of your husband.'

She didn't know what to do. Courtesy demanded that she invite him inside the house, and part of her wanted to. She was really pleased to see him. But another part of her was obscurely afraid of him, wanted him to go, to leave her alone so that she could get on with her new life.

Finally, her ingrained good manners won out over caution. Surely he meant her no harm? She opened the door wider and stood aside.

'Won't you come in?' she asked politely. He nodded and stepped inside. When she had closed the door, shutting out the street noises, the house seemed suddenly very quiet. 'I was just fixing myself a sandwich,' she said to him as they walked down the hall. 'Would you care to join me?'

They were at the door to the kitchen now. She glanced up at him, but couldn't read the expression on his face. He looked tanned and fit, the bright blue eyes as startling as ever, and she noticed he needed a haircut.

'Thank you,' he said. 'I'd like that.'

She didn't know whether to be glad or sorry. He made her nervous, and when he followed her into the kitchen he seemed to fill it with his presence. He stood with his back to her, surveying the large room critically with his architect's eye.

She remembered her first impression of him that day so long ago when she and Armand had driven out to Beaux Champs. She had thought then that he had been too much of everything, and in the confines of the kitchen, alone with him, he seemed more overwhelming than ever.

'Please sit down,' she said with a gesture towards the table by the window. 'I won't be a minute.'

She went to the counter and began making sandwiches, slicing cheese, setting the coffee on to perk, hoping she didn't look too clumsy at the unfamiliar domestic tasks. The nuns had taught her to cook, but it had been over six years since then, six years of idleness.

'So,' he said from behind her, 'what are your plans? Charles tells me you've decided to stay on here, not move out to Beaux Champs with your family.'

He had been discussing her with Charles again, she thought. Somehow the idea made her uncomfortable. Still, Charles was the family lawyer, typically discreet, and would not have revealed any of the details of her financial situation.

She carried the sandwiches to the table and sat down opposite him. 'That's right,' she said. 'This house belongs to me now. I'm going to rent out the upstairs apartment.' He lifted an eyebrow and stared at her. 'I don't suppose you approve,' she rushed on.

'Why shouldn't I approve?' he asked. 'It's your house.'

'I mean from an architect's point of view. You know, it's a fine old house. You probably think I should keep it as it is.'

He shrugged. 'Houses are meant to be lived in. Besides, the place has been remodelled at least once already to make the two self-contained apartments. You won't have to touch it.'

He took a bite of sandwich and chewed thoughtfully for a moment, lounging back comfortably in the oak chair, one arm draped casually over the back. He seemed totally at ease, but Lelia sensed a strange tension in the way his eyes followed her every movement.

She got the coffee and cream, and while she poured, she could feel him looking at her.

'I'm wondering, though,' he said at last, 'why you want to take in a tenant. Won't having a stranger living here interfere with your social commitments?'

She debated for a moment just how far she should confide in him about her plans. Then she gave him a level gaze over the rim of her coffee cup. 'I have no more social commitments,' she said calmly, 'and I need the money.'

He only raised the black eyebrows a hair and cocked his head to one side. Then, 'You're full of surprises today, Lelia.' The blue eyes travelled lightly over the rumpled silk shirt and untidy hair. 'I came by expecting to see the old perfect china doll – expensive, pampered, artifical. And helpless. Instead, I find a real, live, flesh-and-blood woman, who seems quite capable.'

Lelia laughed lightly to cover her embarrassment at his frank and penetrating assessment of her. 'I'm sorry to disappoint you,' she said with a little shrug. 'I've been working.'

He leaned towards her, compelling her to meet his gaze. 'Oh, I'm not disappointed, Lelia,' he said in a low voice. 'I saw that real woman once before. Remember? The day of the storm.'

She flushed deeply and turned her head away. 'That never happened,' she murmured. 'You said so yourself.'

'I lied,' he stated flatly. 'It happened, all right. I know it, and you know it.' He paused. 'That's really why I came today. I wanted to find out if that real woman still existed or was only a hallucination, a figment of my imagination.'

She turned distressed eyes on him. His face was unyielding, like granite. How can he be so cruel? she thought. He knows I don't want to be reminded of that episode. She got up from her chair. She had to get away from him. But before she could take one step, she felt his hand clamp down hard on her arm.

'Let me go,' she said, suddenly afraid of him. 'Why are you doing this to me?'

He stood up, then, and frowned down at her. She turned her head away, unable to face him.

'I'll tell you why, Lelia. It's because you've hidden from the truth about yourself long enough.' He took hold of her chin and forced her head around so that she had to face him. 'I knew it the first time I set eyes on you. That haughty manner and remote, nunlike image never fooled me for a minute. The way you responded to me that day proved it. Admit it.'

What was happening here? Lelia's mind spun around in confusion. How could the man who had been so coolly polite all these months suddenly become so physical, so threatening, so demanding?

'You're frightening me,' she said in a small voice. 'Please let me go.'

Her pleading tone only seemed to inflame him. He put strong hands on her shoulders and shook her. 'You've been a hothouse flower for so long that you've almost lost the capacity to feel,' he ground out.

Still stunned by this display of emotion from a man she had thought of as totally controlled, she gazed up into his eyes, hoping to read something in them that would help her make him understand.

What she saw there almost took her breath away. Instead of hostility, she saw genuine concern. Instead of uncontrolled passion, she saw something almost pleading. She became dimly aware that she, too, had a certain incomprehensible power over him. This realisation steadied her, and suddenly she wasn't afraid of him any more.

'What is it you want from me, Michael?' she asked calmly.

She saw a strange gleam appear in the blue, blue eyes. 'I'll show you what I want,' he murmured triumphantly and the dark head came down.

She closed her eyes and waited. When she realised that he was going to kiss her, the thought flashed through her mind that the wisest course would be simply to allow it, to remain passive and not struggle against him. She made her body go limp and unresisting.

At the first touch of his mouth on hers, however, her resolution vanished. She had expected a brief, punishing onslaught, not this gently, playful pressure. His lips moved warmly, lightly on hers. The hands that had gripped her shoulders came around behind her, enfolding her closely, but not brutally, so that she was even more intensely aware of the hard firm length of his strong body pressed closely to hers than if he had been more demanding.

A pleasant, tingling warmth began to steal through her. The mind she had made deliberately blank betrayed her now. With no intruding thoughts to hinder the blind surge of emotion that filled it, she found herself instinctively responding to him. His lips parted, became more insistent, and the warmth became tongues of fire licking through her bloodstream.

All her latent desire to yield was aroused. Mindless now, her hands crept up around his neck, into his hair, and as she pressed herself closer to him, she felt a shudder run through him, heard a low groan at the back of his throat.

His mouth left hers then, was at her cheek, her ear, her throat, his hands moving restlessly over her back, up under the thin silk blouse, warm and strong on her bare skin.

'Michael,' she whispered. 'Oh, Michael.'

She drank in his heady masculine scent as his shaven cheek rasped lightly against hers, then threw her head back, lost now in the rapture of the moment. This, then, was desire, she thought, this wanting that had the power to banish every other consideration from her mind, where the only reality, the only necessity, was to be held in *these* strong arms, feel *this* mouth on hers, *these* hands on her body.

One hand slid around then to her breast and rested there. At the touch, she gasped and opened her eyes. The blue gaze held her hypnotically as the hand tightened, then began to move gently, the long sensitive fingers curling around the soft fullness.

'Lelia,' he breathed, 'I want you. God, how I've wanted you all these months.' His hand moved now, and still resting on her breast, started to unbutton her blouse. Her head was reeling from the pounding of the blood in her ears, and she made no move to stop him. Somewhere, beneath her mindless surrender, she was dimly aware of a vague feeling of apprehension, a little nagging sense of doubt at what she was doing, what she was allowing him to do.

But by now, she had no power to resist him. She ran her hands up over his chest, along the broad shoulders and up to clasp the strong jaw. Then she lowered her mouth to press her lips into the hollow at the base of his throat, and she could feel the pulse pounding there.

When she moaned deeply, he pulled her to him again, harder this time, his arousal clearly evident to her, and began to slip the blouse off her shoulders.

'You're the most beautiful, desirable woman I've ever known,' he breathed now into her ear. Her blouse was half off by now, and his hands slipped under the waistband of her skirt. 'The first time I set eyes on you I dreamed of holding you like this, touching you like this.' He pulled her closer, so that their bodies were more intimately moulded. 'Every time I saw you with Armand, all I could think of was the beautiful body underneath those elegant dresses. . .'

She stiffened in his arms, and his voice trailed off. Armand, she thought. How could she have forgotten Armand? He had never held her like this, kissed her like this, touched her like this. He had never even seen her like this. What was she doing here, half-undressed in the arms of a virtual stranger, when her own poor, crippled husband had not even been able to look at her without an agony of frustration and thwarted desire?

She drew back. 'Armand,' she said.

Michael only stared at her for a moment. He had sensed her withdrawal immediately at the sound of her dead husband's name.

'Don't, Lelia,' he said at last. 'Don't leave me like that.' He tried to pull her back to him, to kiss her again, but she turned her head away and struggled out of his arms.

She just stood there, so shocked at what she had done, what she had been about to do, that all desire drained out of her. She could only stare at him, aghast.

'Armand,' she whispered again.

Then she began to tremble. She turned her back to him and with a little cry, pulled her blouse together and buttoned it securely again. With shaky steps, she walked over to the kitchen counter and leaned against it until the trembling finally ceased.

Quiet tears began to fall then, stinging her eyes, rolling down her cheeks. She heard him come up behind her, felt his presence close, but not touching her.

'Please go,' she said at last in a weary voice. 'Please.'

'Lelia, listen to me.' Although not without sympathy, his low voice was firm and authoritative. 'Armand is dead.'

She whirled around then. 'Don't you think I know that?' she cried out.

He put a hand out towards her, but when she shrank back from him, quickly withdrew it.

'I'm sorry,' he said. 'I've behaved like a clumsy unfeeling clod. It was too soon. I've rushed you.' He ran a hand through the unruly black hair. 'Can we start over again?'

She looked at him. She had never known a man who appealed to her even remotely the way this one did. But how many men had she known? Her experience was virtually nonexistent.

She loved being in his arms, loved his kisses, the feel of his hands on her, his hard body close to her, but he overwhelmed her. She dimly sensed that if she let him, he would take over and dominate her life just as Armand had done.

'No,' she said at last. 'We can't. I don't want to see you again.'

He frowned. 'That's crazy, and you know it. I realise it's too soon to tell just what it is yet, but there's something between us, something important. You felt it, too. I know you did.'

'I don't know what I felt.' She saw the sceptical look of disbelief on his face. 'You don't understand. How could you? I can't explain it, and even if I tried, you probably wouldn't believe me.'

'Try me,' he said shortly.

Frowning, she searched her mind for the words to convey to him what she felt. She wished he would just leave. His nearness unnerved her. She couldn't think with him standing so close to her. She hated the feelings he aroused in her. She didn't trust them. They would betray her, she knew, into a commitment that would only enslave her again.

But how to make him understand that? He was a man,

free, independent, with a place of his own in the world. She had lived in Armand's shadow so long that she felt she hardly existed.

'I—I—' she began, reddening. Then she swallowed and took a deep breath. 'I have to find out who I am.'

She braced herself for an echo of Armand's taunting laughter, but instead Michael only looked at her gravely, as though he took her statement quite seriously and was turning it over thoughtfully in his mind.

'That's fair enough,' he said at last. 'I can appreciate how you must feel. It's important for all of us to find out who we are. You told me once you married right out of the convent, and I can see that you never got that chance.'

Her tension began to ebb out of her. She could physically feel the tight shoulder muscles relaxing, the fists unclenching. He *did* understand.

'Still,' he went on, 'what I don't see is what that has to do with us.'

'*Us!*' she said, on her guard again. 'There is no "us".'

'The hell there isn't!' His voice cut into the quiet room. 'I wasn't performing all by myself a few minutes ago. You were with me ever step of the way.'

She turned her head away and bit her lip. 'That should never have happened. I'm so ashamed. I hardly know you.'

'That's what I'm trying to tell you, Lelia.' There was a note of exasperation in his voice. 'Let's get to know each other. Forget about your social Mrs Duval image and try just being a woman.' He held up his hands. 'No strings, no commitments. No lovemaking, if you don't want it.' He grinned. 'I'm thirty-four years old and have had my fair share of relationships with women, but I've never forced one of them into anything she didn't want as much as I did.'

And that was just the trouble, she thought miserably. He was *too* appealing, *too* irresistible. It wasn't that she didn't trust him. She didn't trust herself. How could she tell him that?

'It just wouldn't work for me,' she said flatly. 'I'm not ready. It's too soon.'

He made a little gesture of impatience. 'What can I say to convince you?'

'Nothing. There's nothing you can say.'

'Convince me, then,' he said, holding her gaze in his. 'Convince me this does nothing to you.' He took her face in his hands and kissed her, his mouth hard and insistent. 'Or this,' he murmured against her lips. One hand moved to her breast.

In spite of herself, she felt her knees grow weak at the touch of his mouth, his hand. Her heart started to pound wildly. Surely he could feel it, with his hand placed so firmly just over that mad fluttering.

She tore her lips from his and stepped back a pace. 'I don't have to convince you of anything!' she cried. 'Don't you see? You're just like Armand!' She was beside herself now, raving. 'All you want is a puppet, just like he did.'

He reached out a hand to her, but when she shrank back from him, his arms fell to his sides.

'That's not true, Lelia.' His face was white and pinched. He seemed to be making an effort to control himself. 'You know that's not true.'

'You said you never forced yourself on anyone.' She

hardly knew what she was saying now. 'So will you please leave? Now. Please,' she wailed.

She covered her face with her hands and stood there trembling. In a moment, she heard his footsteps as he crossed the room, then down the hall, until finally the front door opened and closed.

When she was quite certain he was really gone, she sat down at the table and stared out of the window for a long time. There was a family of mockingbirds in the redbud tree out in the patio, and she watched them now as they fluttered around the concrete birdbath. The roses were in full bloom. She could cut some and bring them into the house, she thought.

A strange clarity of mind began to replace the wild confusion Michael Feilding's disturbing presence had stirred in her. She wanted to be honest with herself. She knew she couldn't build an authentic life if it was based on a lie.

He was right. She did respond to him, desire him. His kiss did set her heart singing, her pulses racing. She could deny that to him, for the sake of sheer self-preservation, but not to herself. She also liked him, just as a person. He was kind and thoughtful, and seemed genuinely interested in her struggle to grow out of her cocoon. There was also no question that he found her desirable, even beautiful.

She was simply afraid of him. She could see herself getting lost in those blue eyes, those strong arms, that magical mouth, lost before she had even found herself. She would have solved nothing if she leaped now into the same trap she was finally escaping.

Yes, she thought, I like him, I desire him, probably

could even love him, but in gaining him, I would lose
everying else.

CHAPTER SIX

THE FOLLOWING week was hectic, and Lelia hardly had a moment to think about Michael Fielding. On the few occasions when she did sense her thoughts wandering in that direction, she stopped them immediately before they could take hold in her mind. He was gone, she reminded herself, and he wouldn't come back. Not after the way she had rejected him so positively.

The day after his visit, she had her hair cut. She chose an inexpensive hairdressing salon down on Canal Street where she wasn't known, and when she looked at her reflection in the mirror after the operation was over, she hardly recognised herself.

The thick, shiny black hair, unsprayed, unteased, unarranged, fell loosely now almost to her shoulders, where it curled up slightly at the ends. When she ran her hands over it, it felt clean, healthy and full of life.

She spent two whole days drawing up a careful inventory of the contents of the house and making arrangements with a moving company to transfer some of her furniture upstairs. As she had anticipated, there was plenty for both apartments. She had longed to clear out the cluttered ground floor for years anyway. Eventually, she wanted to get rid of the heavy, oppressive draperies, too, she decided as she surveyed the drawing room with a critical eye during the inventory. Put up some sheer curtains, let more light in.

Charles came by late one afternoon. The movers had just left. She had done some light furniture shifting herself and was hot, dusty and tired, her blue jeans and checked cotton shirt grimy and wrinkled.

When she answered the door to him, he just stood there staring at her for several seconds, the hazel eyes wide. Finally, he grinned.

'Have I come to the right house? It is Lelia Duval, isn't it?'

'Come in, Charles,' she said with a nervous laugh. He had never seen her looking so dishevelled, and his shocked stare embarrassed her. 'Have I shattered my image that drastically?'

She shut the door behind him, and they stood in the foyer facing each other. Charles looked big and solid, neat and well-dressed as always in a striped suit.

'I'm glad you stopped by,' she went on, 'I wanted to ask your advice about something. Let's go out in the courtyard. I could use a cool drink right about now.'

Still speechless, Charles followed her through the dining room and out on to the paved courtyard. It was quiet and peaceful, the high brick walls and profuse foliage shutting out the street noises of the busy French Quarter.

'Sit down, Charles, and get that look off your face. You're making me nervous.' She felt vaguely apprehensive. Had she made herself ugly? She still wasn't sure enough of herself to take Charles's reaction in her stride.

He scratched his head and sat down slowly on one of the white wrought-iron chairs, still staring at her in wonderment.

'I can't believe it,' he said when he finally found his

voice. 'You look so. . .' He paused, frowned, then grinned. 'So human.'

She breathed a long sigh. 'Well, that's a relief, anyway. For a minute there you looked as though I'd suddenly grown two heads.'

He shook his head, still stunned. 'I'm sorry, Lelia. I didn't mean to be rude. You look great. More beautiful than ever. Honestly.'

She smiled then. 'I don't know about that. I only know I feel wonderful, really alive.' She blushed. 'How about that drink? Lemonade?'

She went into the kitchen to get the drinks, still a little nervous over her first public appearance, but gratified that Charles seemed to think she looked all right.

She brought out a pitcher and two tumblers and set them down on the glass-topped table. It was quite warm, but the large redbud and mimosa trees cast a pleasant shade, and on the upper terrace a small fountain splashed coolly.

'Have you found a renter yet for the upstairs apartment?' Charles asked.

She frowned. 'I've had several calls, but none of them sounded promising. Even though the two apartments are entirely separate, I feel I should try to get someone I'd be compatible with. It's pretty close quarters.'

Charles sipped his drink and nodded. 'That's wise. I don't think you'll have any trouble finding someone suitable, and there's no rush.'

'What I wanted to ask about, Charles, was whether or not you can continue to help me.'

He raised his eyebrows and leaned forward across the table towards her. 'Of course, I'll help you, Lelia. How could you doubt it? I'm your friend.'

'I know that, Charles,' she said quickly, 'and I really appreciate all you've done. I mean help me professionally, as a legal adviser.' Her eyes clouded over. 'You know, Tante Amalie and I didn't part on the best of terms.'

He gave her a sharp look. 'Are you anticipating a legal battle?'

'Oh, no. Nothing like that. At least, I hope not.' She thought of the furniture Tante Amalie had taken that by rights belong to her. 'I don't think they'll make any trouble for me, and I certainly don't want to make any for them.'

Charles leaned back in his chair. 'Well, then, I see no reason not to represent you legally if you need my advice. The only conceivable problem that could arise is if there became a conflict of interest.' He grinned. 'And in that case, the choice of which client to represent would be mine. I could always disqualify myself from acting for Amalie.'

'Oh, no, Charles. I'd never want you to do that.' She knew the Duval family was one of his firm's wealthiest clients. 'Besides, all I'd ask you to do is draw up a lease and maybe help me sell some furniture and jewellery.'

He spread his hands. 'No problem. Any time you need me, just give me a call.'

They sat in companionable silence then for some time. The family of mockingbirds was busy again at the bird bath, and a striking bright red cardinal flashed across from the mimosa tree into the fountain.

Lelia's mind was greatly relieved by Charles's assurance of help. She was so ignorant of business affairs, she thought, and knowing that she could count on this kind, sturdy man's assistance gave her spirits a decided lift.

Charles's voice broke the stillness. 'Did you know that Michael Fielding was in town a few days ago?'

She jumped a little and gave him a quick glance. His voice had been casual. Too casual, she thought. Did he suspect that their relationship had been more personal than it appeared on the surface? She felt herself reddening and looked away.

'Yes,' she said, trying to sound offhand. 'He stopped by briefly one afternoon. A condolence call. He said he was just passing through New Orleans on his way to Houston. It was kind of him to call,' she ended up lamely.

Charles gave her a long, appraising look. 'He seems very—interested—in you,' he commented.

'I think,' Lelia replied drily, 'that he's a man who is probably interested in a great many women.'

'Why do you say that?'

Lelia shrugged. 'Just an impression.' She thought of the night of the dinner party and how the women had clustered around him. 'Am I wrong?'

Charles laughed at that. 'I don't really know his personal habits that well,' he replied evasively. 'I do know that women find him attractive. Don't you? It would be only natural for you to. . .' He broke off. 'You know what I mean.'

'I don't think about it,' she stated flatly and shifted uncomfortably in her chair. His question struck a little too close to home.

'He's an interesting guy,' Charles went on, toying idly with his glass tumbler. 'Has a worldwide reputation as a restoration architect, and really knows his stuff.'

'He seems to,' Lelia murmured. 'He did wonders with Beaux Champs.' She refilled their glasses just for something to do. Now that the conversation had shifted away from her own relationship with Michael Fielding, she found she was interested to learn more about him.

'The funny thing is,' Charles continued, 'he doesn't have to work at all. He told me once he started his career as a hobby. His father was a prominent Philadelphia lawyer—I know the firm well—and both his parents came from wealthy families.'

'He must have money of his own, then,' she remarked.

Charles shrugged. 'I would certainly imagine so. His parents are both dead and he was an only child.' He chuckled. 'He said his father was quite upset when he decided to major in art history and architecture at Harvard instead of taking up the law, but apparently Michael's success convinced the old man he'd chosen the right field and they were reconciled before he died.'

'If he's that well off,' Lelia said lightly, 'it must bother him to be treated like a paid employee in his work.' She recalled Armand's haughty, patronising attitude towards him.

Charles laughed. 'Oh, not Michael. I've never known anyone who cared less what people thought of him or how they treated him.'

Lelia could well imagine that. She remembered the amused look on his face that day when Armand had emphasised so pointedly the fact that he was Michael's employer, and the way he had fit in so easily at the dinner party later.

'Does he spend all his time travelling?' she asked now.

'Surely he must have a home somewhere.'

'I think he still keeps up his family's place in Philadelphia and considers it his home base. Although once he told me he was looking for a house here.'

Lelia's eyes widened. 'Here? You mean in New Orleans?'

Charles gave her a sharp look. 'Yes,' he said slowly. Then, 'You seem very curious about the man for someone who isn't interested.'

She forced out a laugh. 'Oh, Charles, don't be silly. I'm not looking for an involvement with *any* man, much less one as dangerous as I think Michael Fielding must be.'

'That's a pretty sweeping statement, Lelia.' He reached across the table and put a hand on hers. 'Does that include me?'

She didn't know how to answer him. She valued his friendship, his advice, his help, and liked him very much, but that was all. She didn't want to hurt him, but to be fair, she had to be honest with him.

'Right now, yes. It does.' He quickly withdrew his hand and she gave him a pleading look. 'It isn't you, Charles,' she said in a low voice. 'It's just that I'm not ready for anything like that. Please try to understand.'

'Of course,' he began stiffly.

Then the front doorbell rang. 'Excuse me,' she said, and jumped up to answer it, glad of the interruption.

Charles followed her. 'It's time I left, anyway. Call me when you decide what to do about the furniture and jewellery. I think an auction consignment would be your best bet.'

When she opened the front door, she saw a tall, heavily

built grey-haired woman standing there. She gazed gravely down at Lelia, then up at Charles, without speaking. Charles gave her a look and a brief nod.

'Goodbye, then, Lelia,' he said. 'I'll be in touch.'

'Goodbye, Charles. And thank you for everything.' When he was gone, she turned to the woman. 'Yes? May I help you?'

'Mrs Duval?' The voice was low and melodic, a contrast to the stern features. Lelia nodded. The woman went on. 'My name is Madame Constanza Fiorini. I've come about the apartment.'

Lelia gave her a swift, appraising glance. Madame Fiorini? The name was familiar, but she couldn't quite place it. She had talked to several prospective tenants already and rejected each one. The only criterion she had to go on was her own instinct. She knew she didn't want a man living there at all. That was an easy decision. Of the women, one was too young and scatterbrained, another talked too much, another seemed too nosy, and so on, until finally she began to wonder if she would ever find anyone just right.

Madame Fiorini stood at the door quietly waiting. She had an extraordinary presence, Lelia thought, very composed, very poised, with sharp intelligent eyes that didn't miss a thing.

'Come in,' she said at last. 'I'll show you the apartment.'

As the two women walked through the rooms, they discussed lease terms, rental payment and other business matters. Lelia found Madame Fiorini easy to talk to and knowledgeable about such things as utility arrangements, damage deposits and open-end leases.

When they had finished the tour and were standing at the top of the stairs, Madame Fiorini turned to Lelia and looked steadily at her for a moment. Then she said, 'Before you make up your mind, I must tell you a little about myself. There is one serious drawback to my tenancy you should know about.'

Lelia's heart sank. The more they talked, the more she liked the tall woman with her calm, confident manner. For a large woman, she carried herself gracefully, with almost practised movements. She asked intelligent questions, none of them personal, and her comments were sharp and to the point.

An ideal tenant, Lelia had decided. Now there was a serious drawback. She sighed. 'Come down to the drawing room,' she said, 'and we can talk about it.

When they had settled themselves on a sofa in the drawing room, Madame Fiorini turned her calm dark eyes on Lelia.

'I am a singer,' she said. She smiled for the first time. 'Before your day, I'm afraid.'

Of course, Lelia thought. That's where she'd heard the name. She was—had been—a famous opera star. 'I've heard of you, though,' she murmured. 'I just didn't make the connection.'

The other woman nodded. 'I no longer sing professionally, of course,' she went on, 'but I do give lessons. That is, I coach carefully selected professionals.' She smiled again. 'Musicians are noisy creatures, and practice work is boring to listen to. I have a piano. A loud one, a concert grand. I don't know how good the soundproofing is here, but I believe these old houses were very solidly built.'

Lelia bit her lip, thinking this over. She had never heard any noise from upstairs when Tante Amalie and Blanche lived there, but then they were two very quiet women. What would it be like to have the sounds of music coming down at all hours of the day or night?

'I don't know,' she said at last. 'Would you have specific times for your lessons?'

'Oh, yes. I only take a few pupils at a time, and always work in the afternoon.' She sighed. 'I know it's a great deal to ask, and you won't offend me if you turn me down. I love the apartment, however. It's perfect to me. Houses in the French Quarter are very rare, you know, and I am determined to live here. One recently came up for sale, on Dauphine Street, but someone else bought it before my agent could even make an offer.' She shrugged. 'Perhaps I'll have to look further out after all.'

'No,' Lelia said, making up her mind. 'I'd like to give it a try, anyway.' This woman was perfect for her, she thought, and maybe the noise wouldn't penetrate through the thick ceiling or, if it did, she might not mind it. 'Shall we say a month's trial?'

Madame Fiorini thought this over. 'Very well,' she said at last. 'A month.' She stood up and held out a hand. 'Thank you, Mrs Duval. You've been very kind.'

'When do you want to move in?' Lelia asked as they walked back out to the front door.'

'As soon as possible.'

'All right. I'll have Charles—my lawyer—draw up a lease right away. As soon as it's signed, you can move in.'

Two days later, Charles had prepared the lease agreement, and both women signed it. Charles had taken immediately to Madame Fiorini and seemed delighted that Lelia would have such a compatible tenant.

It became apparent after only a few weeks that the arrangement suited them both perfectly. Even though they rarely saw each other, Lelia found it a comfort to have someone living in the house with her.

With the rent money Madame paid her, Lelia's anxieties about her financial situation were eased, and she arranged her schedule so that she would be gone in the afternoons when the pupils came for their lessons.

She had become deeply involved in volunteer work at a retarded children's centre, and had committed herself to spend three hours every afternoon helping to care for a group of six-year-olds.

She rarely thought about Armand any more, and as time passed and the shock of his death quietly ebbed away, it gradually came to her that the Armand she had loved and married had been virtually dead for years anyway. A bitter, self-pitying stranger had taken his place, and she looked back now on the five years of their marriage as a painful imprisonment for them both.

Gone at last, too, was the guilt she had suffered over her part in the accident that crippled him. She had tried her best to be a good wife to him and had given him five years of patient, loyal, uncomplaining obedience. The slate was wiped clean now.

As the days and weeks passed, her life settled into a pleasant routine. Occasionally, she found her thoughts wandering back to that last encounter with Michael Fielding, and twice she thought she saw him on the street when she was walking home from the retarded children's centre. However, she remained firm in her decision not to even consider a relationship with a man, and so dismissed him from her mind.

Charles had been gone on vacation for most of July, and Lelia missed him. He had been an enormous help to her in the beginning, right after Armand's death. It was he who had made all the arrangments for her to sell several pieces of her jewellery and the more fragile pieces of furniture she didn't want.

One morning, Lelia invited Madame down for coffee for the first time. It was quite apparent by now, that she intended to guard her privacy as zealously as Lelia herself, so there was no reason why they shouldn't meet occasionally.

July in New Orleans was deadly, and they sat out in the paved courtyard under the welcome shade of the giant mimosa tree. It was only ten o'clock and already the heat and humidity were becoming oppressive. Mornings were the only times of day in the summer that it was bearable to be out of doors, away from the incessant air-conditioning inside, and Lelia liked to take advantage of it.

'This is very pleasant, Mrs Duval,' Madame said with a flourish towards the garden. The roses were in full, glorious bloom, and the fountain on the upper terrace splashed gently, cooling the air.

'Yes,' Lelia replied. 'It's a lovely courtyard, isn't it? The house has been in my husband's family for generations, and this is all as it was originally planned by the first Duval. Even the brick walls are the same.' She smiled. 'And please call me Lelia.'

Madame nodded and sipped her coffee. 'Lelia. A lovely name.' She gave her a thoughtful look, as if debating within herself, then said, 'I believe your husband died recently.' It was more a question than a statement.

Lelia flushed and lowered her eyes. 'Yes,' she said shortly. 'Just a few months ago.'

'Forgive me, my dear,' Madame said quickly. 'I don't mean to pry.' She laughed, a deep rich sound. 'You and I, I think, are both women who value our privacy and independence.'

'It's not that,' Lelia smiled to reassure her. 'I don't mind talking about it.'

'You still miss him, though.'

Lelia frowned. 'No.' She spread her hands, and gave Madame a long look. 'I don't.' She sighed. 'He wasn't happy the way he was.'

Madame nodded. 'I understand he was confined to a wheelchair and in poor health. Very sad. But if one can rise above such an infirmity. . .' She shrugged her heavy shoulders lightly.

'Armand wasn't able to do that. He. . .' She hesitated, then went on in a low voice. 'Sometimes I think he wanted to die.'

'Well,' Madame said firmly, 'life is for the living, isn't it? You are getting on with your life quite capably, it seems to me. You mentioned that you were working with retarded children. Tell me about it.'

Lelia's face lit up. 'They are so lovable. Since they understand so little, they're virtually untouched by life and have an air of innocence that makes them very appealing. They love music, and I play for them, try to get them to sing along with me.'

Madame smiled. 'You have a kind heart to be so drawn

by another's helplessness. Good works without love is almost worthless. What did Saint Paul say?' She thought a moment, then quoted: '"Though I speak with the tongues of men and of angels and have not love, I am but a tinkling cymbal or a sounding gong."'

The doorbell rang just then, and the two women looked at each other in surprise. Then they both started laughing.

Lelia jumped to her feet. 'Speaking of gongs. Excuse me. I'll be right back.'

Madame stood up and drained the last of her coffee. 'I must go prepare for my pupils. It's been very pleasant. I hope you will invite me again.'

They walked companionably together into the house. At the foyer, Lelia opened the door and her face lit up when she saw Charles Donaldson standing there.

'Charles, how nice to see you. Come in.' She shut the door behind him. 'You remember Madame Fiorini.'

'Of course.' Charles looked up at the other woman. She had started upstairs to her own apartment and turned now to greet him.

She nodded graciously, an imperious figure standing there on the wide staircase, one hand on the carved banister, just as though she were making a grand entrance in a scene from opera.

'Mr Donaldson,' she said. She turned to Lelia. 'Thank you again for the coffee, Lelia.'

'Not at all. We'll do it again soon.'

When she was gone, Lelia turned to Charles. Her dark eyes were sparkling, her face alight with pleasure.

'Charles, it's wonderful to see you.' She took his arm. 'Come inside and tell me about your vacation.'

'I'll have to go away more often if I can count on this kind of reception when I get back.' He smiled down at her as they walked through the house. His tone was light, but there was an underlying seriousness in the kind hazel eyes. 'You look wonderful, Lelia.'

They were in the drawing room now, and Charles stopped short. His mouth fell open as he gazed around at the transformed room. Lelia had cleared out much of the furniture and had finally replaced the heavy damask at the windows with sheer curtains and short casement cloth draperies.

'I can't believe it,' he said at last. 'It's a different room, airier, lighter—and far more liveable.'

Lelia breathed a sigh of relief. It had seemed almost sacrilegious to make such sweeping changes in the elegant room, but since she owned the house now and she was the one who had to live in it, she had told herself, she had the right to do what she pleased.

'I'm so glad you approve,' she said. 'I've been a little worried.'

'Of course I approve,' he said warmly, his eyes sweeping the room again. Then he laughed. 'However, I don't know what Amalie and Blanche will say.'

'I doubt very much if they'll be visiting at Chartres Street,' she replied drily. 'They don't approve of any of my plans, much less changing the house around.'

Charles raised an eyebrow. 'Like that, huh?'

Lelia nodded solemnly. 'Like that.' Then, as if in unison, they smiled at each other. 'So you can see,' she went on, 'I'm not too worried about what they think.' Then she added, 'Although I suppose Michael Fielding would be horrified.'

Charles gave her a quick look. 'Don't be too sure. He's always said houses were meant to be lived in.' He hesitated. 'Did you know he was in town?'

Lelia's smile faded. 'No, I didn't.' She recalled the times she thought she had caught a glimpse of him on the street. Maybe it had been him after all.

'Yes,' Charles went on. 'He's bought a house on Dauphine Street.'

'To live in?' Lelia asked carefully. Dauphine Street was only three blocks away.

'Well, to restore anyway. I don't think his plans are firm.'

'Madame Fiorini almost bought a house on Dauphine. I wonder if it's the same one.'

Charles shrugged. 'Could be. Old houses in the French Quarter are hard to come by.' He paused. 'Well, Lelia, I'd better get to the office. I'm sure the work will be piled sky high after a month's absence.'

'Of course,' Lelia murmured distractedly, as they walked back into the foyer. She was disturbed by the news that Michael Fielding lived so close to her, but she didn't want Charles to know that. 'I'm glad you stopped by.'

At the door, he turned to her and gave her a grave look. 'What I really came for was to ask you if you'd have dinner with me Saturday night.' She couldn't hide a troubled look, and he hurried on. 'I don't mean to rush you, Lelia. If it's too soon after Armand's death, just say so.'

She frowned and looked down at her feet. 'It's not that, Charles.' She sighed. 'I was just thinking today that in a sense, Armand really died the day of the accident.

Everything after that was only a long purgatory. For both of us.' She looked up at him. 'I just don't want. . .' She stopped. She didn't want to hurt him, nor did she want to presume more than he intended by his invitation.

'I understand,' he put in quickly, 'I really do. We're friends, that's all. I like being with you.'

She brightened then. It would be fun to go out to dinner. Her social life before Armand's death had consisted exclusively of society engagements at private homes. Armand hated restaurants. He always felt people stared at him in his wheelchair. Since his death she had gone nowhere.

'Yes,' she said. 'I'd like that, Charles.'

'Good.' He put his hand on the door. 'Where would you like to go? Antoine's? Tortorici's? Pat O'Brien's? New Orleans is famous for its restaurants, so we have our pick of the best.'

She thought a moment. 'Antoine's,' she said. 'I've never been there.'

'Antoine's it is, then.' He was obviously pleased at her acceptance. 'I'll make reservations for Saturday night and pick you up at seven.'

He left then, and when Lelia had shut the door behind him, she leaned back against it staring into space. Had she made a mistake in agreeing to go out to dinner with Charles? He seemed to understand and accept that she didn't want an involvement of any kind with him. He knew she valued his friendship. But would that be enough for him?

She sighed and started through the house and out on to the courtyard to clear away the coffee things. It wasn't until she was back in the kitchen, rinsing out the cups, that she remembered what Charles had told her about Michael.

Her heart lurched at the thought of him. She turned off the tap and stood at the sink, her hands braced on the counter top, deep in thought.

It had been here, in this very room, that she had seen him last. A slow warm flush crept up her body and over her face as she recalled his voice, his touch, his kiss. Living so close by now, she was bound to see him. It was amazing that she hadn't already, except for those few questionable glimpses in the street.

Then, startled, she thought, perhaps *he's* avoiding *me*! She wouldn't blame him after the way she had dismissed him the last time they met. Yet, what else could she have done? She had already admitted to herself that she found him compellingly attractive, but still he frightened her. He had awakened feelings in her she never knew existed, feelings she wasn't prepared to deal with.

And that was the trouble. She wasn't afraid of him, but of what he might make her feel and do. She liked her new life. She had put the past firmly behind her and was just becoming comfortable with herself, her home, her work. The director of the children's agency had recently hinted at the possibility of a paying job in the office aside from her volunteer work. The extra money would be most welcome, as well as the satisfaction that comes from being paid for what she did.

She was making it on her own, and that's all she really wanted. Wasn't it? Somehow, the sudden intrusion of Michael Fielding into her thoughts again, just when she thought she had successfully forgotten him, made everything else seem a little flat and colourless.

By that afternoon, deeply involved with the children at the centre, Lelia had forgotten her fears. Listening to their happy laughter and clapping hands, encouraging them to sing along with her at the piano, she felt safe. She was needed here. This was where she belonged.

CHAPTER SEVEN

ANTOINE'S was smaller and more crowded than Lelia had imagined it would be, but still had an indefinable air of Old World elegance.

She sat across from Charles now in the high-backed chair sipping a mild after-dinner drink she couldn't remember the name of that Charles had insisted she try. It was more like a dessert than a drink.

Charles had been staring at her for some time, toying with his drink. Finally he spoke.

'Did I tell you, Lelia, that you're looking very lovely tonight?'

She laughed. 'Yes, Charles, you did. Several times.'

'Sorry,' he said.

'Oh, don't be. I love it.'

She felt herself that she looked her best tonight, and the soft lighting of the crowded restaurant enhanced the effect. She had chosen one of the simplest of her old designer dresses tucked away at the back of her wardrobe. It was made of sheer silk georgette in a creamy white shade, gathered at the shoulders and waist, and with a strapless underslip.

Her black hair hung loosely about her small dark face, and with the heightened colour of her skin these days, she needed no make-up except a light lipstick. Her eyes sparkled with excitement, darting everywhere so as not to miss anything.

123

Charles lit a cigar. 'Do you mind?'

'No. I like it.'

He sighed contentedly. 'I hope you enjoyed that dinner as much as I did.'

A piano tinkled pleasantly in the distance over the hum of conversation. 'I'm enjoying everything, Charles. I don't know when I've had such a pleasant evening.'

It was true. This was her first night out since Armand's death, and the first ever on a real date. She looked at Charles. Date? she thought. Perhaps. But a safe one.

Charles glanced at his watch. 'It's still early, only a little after ten. Would you like to go on somewhere else for a drink? Maybe we could catch one of the shows on Bourbon Street, or find a place to dance.'

Lelia considered. Bourbon Street was lined with raucous nightclubs that catered mainly to tourists. During the season, all the doors to the sidewalk were left open, so that not only was the street one grand cacophony of conflicting strains of jazz music, but one could see the dancers—mostly topless—gyrating on top of the wide wooden bars inside.

'I'm not sure I'm ready for Bourbon Street,' she said dubiously.

Charles laughed. 'Nor I.' He thought a minute. 'Let's see. There's Pat O'Brien's on St Peter Street. It's not far, and I think they have dancing.'

Lelia demurred. She wasn't sure she was ready for that, either. 'Won't it be awfully crowded?'

At that moment, out of the corner of her eye, she noticed a striking couple coming towards them out of the bar. She drew in her breath when she saw that the man was Michael Fielding, tall and imposing in a dark suit, his head bent to the beautiful blonde girl at his side.

Karen Swenson, Lelia thought, and wondered about the absent husband and Michael's rule concerning married women.

She turned her head away and fumbled in her bag, hoping they wouldn't see her. Charles's back was towards them, but they had to pass by their table on their way out.

As luck would have it, just at the critical moment, Charles turned his head to signal for the waiter. His eyes lit up.

'Michael,' he called.

The tall dark man's eyes moved to Charles, then flicked across to Lelia, widening just a little. He spoke to Karen, then they both walked to the table.

'How are you, Charles?' came the deep voice, as the two men shook hands. Then he looked directly at her. 'Lelia, it's nice to see you again.' He turned to the blonde girl. 'I believe you've met Karen.'

Lelia nodded, murmuring a greeting. Charles seemed to know her, too, and Lelia wondered where they had met. What was she doing here in New Orleans?

Charles was standing now, talking to them, and Lelia glanced covertly at the girl while they chatted. She certainly was strikingly looking, deeply tanned, dressed in a low-cut, figure-hugging black dress that was really no more than a slip.

Then Lelia blanched and gave a sudden start as she heard Charles inviting them to sit down at their table. Michael gave her a quick, enquiring look. She smiled courteously, too well brought up to be rude, and before she knew what was happening, Charles had seated Karen at the chair next to him, sat down beside her, and Michael took the chair next to Lelia.

'Lelia and I were just debating where to go next,' Charles was saying. 'We decided to bypass Bourbon Street, maybe try Pat O'Brien's.'

While Charles and Michael discussed the subject, Lelia tried to concentrate on the conversation. Apparently, it had been tacitly decided that whatever they did, it would be together. She wondered if she should plead a headache, ask Charles to take her home.

'I know an out-of-the-way place near Lake Pont-chartrain,' she heard Michael say. 'The Lakeside Inn. Not too crowded.'

'Of course,' said Charles, who lived out that way. 'I know it well.' He turned to Lelia. 'What about it? Want to give it a try?'

Michael hadn't even glanced her way since he sat down. He seemed remote, almost indifferent. Perhaps there was nothing to fear from him after all. Her heart had leapt at the first sight of him, but his casual manner towards her since then reassured her.

'That would be fine,' she agreed carefully.

It was decided to take both cars. As they drove out Gentilly Road to Elysian Fields Avenue, past the city park and along Bayou St John, Lelia fought down a vague sense of unease. Charles was silent by her side, concentrating on the heavy Saturday night traffic. The car radio was playing a popular tune.

There's no need to be nervous, she told herself. She was safe with Charles, and whatever had passed between her and Michael two months ago was best forgotten. He certainly seemed to have put it out of his mind, and he appeared to have eyes only for the beautiful Karen.

His manner towards Lelia the rest of the evening was exactly the same. He never once, by a look or a gesture or a word, conveyed the impression that his interest in her was now or had ever been anything more than friendly.

Even when they danced, he held her at a distance. His arm around her waist was loose, and the large hand held hers lightly, carelessly. She began to seriously wonder if she had dreamed that whole disturbing episode in her kitchen that day when she had come so close to allowing her own passion to betray her.

'Charles tells me you've bought a house,' she said while they danced. He gave her an odd look. She rushed on. 'I hope it wasn't a secret. Charles is always so discreet, it never occurred to me he might be talking out of turn.'

'No,' he said. 'No secret.' The music had stopped and they began to make their way back to the table. 'I'm just a little surprised he mentioned it to you.'

She felt his hand at her waist, guiding her across the crowded floor. His touch was impersonal, a mere courtesy, and gradually her earlier apprehensions about spending the evening with him vanished. She began to thaw, to enjoy herself.

'Do you know the house?' he asked as he seated her at their table. Charles and Karen were still dancing, and they were alone. 'It's the old Bienville house in Dauphine Street.'

'Oh, yes, of course. It's a lovely place.' She smiled. 'In fact, I think you stole it out from under my tenant.'

He raised his eyebrows. 'Tenant?'

'Yes, don't you remember? I told you I was. . .' She broke off, flushing, and took a quick sip of her drink to cover her confusion. She was reminding him, she realised, of an encounter she wanted to forget.

'That's right,' he said easily, turning and signalling the waitress. 'How is it working out?'

'Quite well.' The waitress appeared. Lelia shook her head at Michael's enquiring look, and he ordered another Scotch and water for himself. 'Her name is Constanza Fiorini.' She smiled. '*Madame* Fiorini. A former opera star. We get along beautifully.'

Karen and Charles joined them, then, and they, too ordered another drink. Micahel put his arm casually along the back of the blonde girl's chair. He didn't touch her, but the gesture was intimate, even protective. Lelia wondered again just what their relationship was and what Karen was doing in New Orleans.

As if he could read her thoughts, Michael said, 'Karen is here in town for a while to help me with the restoration work on the new house.'

It was on the tip of Lelia's tongue to ask just what kind of 'help' the beautiful blonde was providing, but she caught herself and heard Karen's low husky voice.

'Actually,' she said with a little laugh, 'I'm really only a glorified dogsbody — seamstress, paperhanger, upholsterer—but my boss likes to make my job sound more important than it really is.'

Michael laughed. 'That's not true.' He gave her an affectionate look and they smiled at each other. 'Your help is invaluable on all my projects, and you know it.'

Lelia felt a small prick of annoyance at this friendly banter. She glanced at Karen's left hand. A wide gold wedding band was on her ring finger. She wanted to ask about her husband, but didn't dare.

'Will you be in town long?' Charles asked.

Karen shrugged her tanned shoulders. 'As long as I'm needed. Perhaps another week. Michael has several projects going around the country. We take turns popping in on them to see how they're coming along.'

Once again, Lelia wondered about the absent Mr Swenson.

'Then perhaps you'll be able to come to a small party I'm having at my place next Saturday night.' He turned to Lelia. 'I haven't told you yet. I'm giving myself a birthday party and hope you'll come, too.' He sighed dramatically. 'We poor bachelors have no one else to do these things for us, you know.' His mouth drooped pathetically.

'Charles!' Lelia exclaimed. 'Of course I'll come. I wouldn't miss it.' She laughed. 'Poor Charles. All alone in the world.' She turned to the others. 'With only half the female population of New Orleans after him.'

Charles casually reached over and took her hand in his. 'I hadn't noticed that. What about the other half?'

'They're probably after Michael,' Karen said lightly. She turned to Charles. 'If I'm still here I'd love to come to your party.'

It was almost midnight when the party broke up. Lelia had enjoyed the evening more than she would have thought possible, and as they walked out into the car park of the inn together, teasing Charles and trying to guess his age, she felt as though she was beginning to catch up with the light-hearted youth she had somehow missed out on.

Michael had parked his car, a grey Peugeot, near the inn, and the two couples said goodnight there under the tall light standard illuminating that part of the lot. Charles' car was parked farther out, and he and Lelia walked towards it through the balmy evening. She thought she had never felt so happy and carefree.

There was a crescent moon in the black sky, and the brightly twinkling stars seemed close enough to reach out and touch.

'Did you have a good time, Lelia?' Charles asked. He held her hand lightly.

She turned shining eyes on him. 'Wonderful, Charles. It was such fun.'

They had reached his car now and Charles got out his keys. 'I'm glad,' he said. 'I like to see you happy.'

He gave her a long look in the moonlight. She could barely make out his features, but something in his tone made her draw back, pull her hand away from his.

He turned abruptly, then, and unlocked the passenger door. Just as she was about to get inside, she heard him utter a sharp oath.

'What is it, Charles?'

He was standing beside the car, staring down at the rear tyres. Bewildered, she watched him as he moved all the way around, inspecting each one. When he came back to her, she could hear his heavy breathing. His anger was almost palpable.

'Someone's put a nail through every damned tyre,' he ground out.

'Oh, Charles, how terrible. Who would do such a thing?'

He shrugged and sighed in exasperation. 'Who knows?

Kids, I suppose. Don't know what to do with themselves in the summertime.' He glared down at the ground, deep in thought. 'Hell, we'd better go back inside and call a taxi.'

Just then, the dark Peugeot came up alongside them, and Michael leaned his head out the window. 'What's up?' he called.

Charles went over to him and with a loud voice and angry gestures explained what had happened.

'I can't do anything about it tonight,' he ended up clearly disgusted. 'I live just up the way on Lark Shore Drive, and I'll have my garage come and pick it up in the morning.'

It was agreed then that Michael would drop Charles off at his house and take Lelia home. They climbed into the back seat.

'Sorry about this, Lelia,' Charles said when he got out in front of his house. 'But you're in good hands.'

'Don't worry about me, Charles,' Lelia said quickly. 'I just feel bad about what happened to your car.'

'I'll call you soon.' He said goodnight then and left.

It was a short ride back to town, and Lelia's thoughts were taken up with poor Charles and his dilemma. He and Michael had agreed that the tyres could probably be resealed, but it was a most annoying inconvenience.

They were back in the French Quarter now, and when Michael pulled the car up to the kerb, Lelia automatically opened the door and got out of the back seat, where she had been sitting alone since Charles left.

It wasn't until she was out on the pavement, still crowded with people even after midnight, that she realised they were not parked in front of the house on

Charles Street, but at the Monteleone Hotel, and that Karen had also got out of the car and was standing on the pavement beside her, her door still open.

Michael was leaning across from the driver's seat. 'Goodnight, Karen,' he called. 'I'll see you on Monday.' He grinned. 'That is, unless you want to work tomorrow.'

'No thanks, boss. Not in my contract.' She turned to Lelia and held out a hand. 'It was nice to see you again, Lelia. I hope we'll meet again.'

Utterly confused by now, Lelia could only murmur something incomprehensible and take the proffered hand. Why had Michael taken Karen home first? Did he expect her to walk to Chartres Street now? She had naturally thought that he and Karen would drop her off, then go to his house together, where she assumed Karen was staying.

Karen was still holding the door open, obviously expecting Lelia to get in beside Michael. She glanced down at him. There was a quizzical, unreadable look on his face.

'Get in, Lelia,' he said.

She obeyed. The door slammed shut, and the car pulled away from the kerb into the heavy flow of traffic.

She sat stiffly, as far over on her side of the seat as it was possible to get. Her hands clutched her bag tightly in her lap, and she stared straight ahead, her face wooden.

What was going on here? She had been so sure all evening that Michael and Karen had a more intimate relationship than that of employer and employee. Yet, looking back, she could recall no word or look or gestures passing between them that would bear out that conclusion.

As they drove the few blocks from the hotel to her house, she glanced surreptitiously at him from time to time out of the corner of her eye. His attention seemed to be fully concentrated on manoeuvring through the traffic.

It occurred to her again what an attractive man he was. The dark hair was well-cut and neatly combed. His strong straight nose, fine mouth and firm chin presented a striking profile. More than that, the ease with which he handled the car, his very posture, relaxed yet alert, gave off a powerful impression of grace and strength.

Had the whole evening been a plot, she wondered, to get her alone? The moment that thought formed in her head, she dismissed it as paranoid. The meeting at Antoine's, the damage to Charles's car had to be accidental.

They were in front of her house now. She started to fumble with the door handle. 'Thank you for the lift,' she mumbled, silently cursing the mysterious latch that simply would not open. She couldn't look at him, and her heart was fluttering erratically.

Then she heard him get out of the car and saw him come around the front to her side. The door opened, and she stepped out on to the pavement beside him. What would he do now? she wondered in dismay. Would he expect her to invite him inside, try to kiss her?

He took her lightly by the arm and led her up the short path to her own front door. When she found the door key in her bag, she looked up at him with a forced, polite smile. In the dim glow of the porch light burning on one side, his face was grave, expressionless.

He took the key from her, unlocked the door and

pushed it open. Then, when she stepped inside and turned to face him, he handed her back her key and nodded briefly.

'Goodnight, then, Lelia,' he said. 'It's been a pleasant evening.'

'Yes,' she murmured hastily. 'Very pleasant. Thank you again for the lift.'

He turned then and walked away from her down the path to the car, one hand in his jacket pocket, his gait unhurried and graceful.

Lelia shut the door, locked it, and leaned back against it. Her heart was still beating rapidly, and she closed her eyes until it slowed to a normal pace.

She walked slowly down the hall to her bedroom, trying to make up her mind what was the proper attitude to take towards Michael's odd behaviour. She was relieved, of course, she told herself. But what did it mean?

He seemed to have taken her at her word, to have accepted the fact that she didn't want an emotional involvement with him, and that was good. Wasn't it?

She undressed, washed, put on her nightgown and got into bed. The heavy canopy was gone now, and the stiff draperies at the windows. The room seemed lighter, airier, fresher. She had been sleeping well.

Tonight, however, she was restless. Unused to night-life, she attributed it to the stimulting evening, and her concern over Charles's car.

Perhaps he had lost interest in her. Wasn't that what she wanted? Of course. Then why, she asked herself as she changed her position for the tenth time, did she feel so let down?

In the week that followed, Lelia didn't have either the time or the inclination to pursue that fruitless line of thinking. The next morning she had awakened with the puzzle still on her mind, but by the time she had dressed and walked to the Basilica for Mass and back, she was able to dismiss it from her mind, deciding that both the reasons she had come up with for Michael's behaviour were probably correct. He obviously was taking her at her word, and as a consequence was turning his attentions elsewhere.

She still had a lot of clearing out to do in the house, and enjoyed making her own decisions as to what to keep and what to sell. She had had no word at all from either Amalie or Blanche since they left Chartres Street, and so assumed her activities were of no interest to them. She was too caught up in her new life to miss them. Madame Fiorini and the children at the centre gave her all the company she needed.

Charles called in the middle of the week to tell her his tyres had been repaired and to confirm his invitation to his birthday party.

'Now that the car is in working order again, I'll be able to drive into town and pick you up Saturday night.'

'Charles, I won't hear of it,' she protested. 'I'm perfectly capable of driving out to your place by myself. You'll have plenty to do without chauffeuring me.'

Charles was dubious. 'Are you sure? I don't like to ask you to do that?'

'You're not asking me, I'm telling you. Now, don't argue. I'm not a hothouse flower, you know.'

'Not any more,' he agreed fervently. 'It amazes me, Lelia, how someone as sheltered as you were all your life can pitch in the way you've done and become so independent.'

She laughed. 'I may have been sheltered, but I was also taught that when you had to do something difficult you didn't sit and whine about it, you just did it. Remember, I wasn't raised in a close-knit family situation. The nuns are very independent women.'

'Just don't get too independent,' he said in a bantering tone. 'You're not a nun, after all, and you're still quite young. You could marry again, have a family.'

'It'll be a long time before I even think about anything like that,' she aid firmly. The subject made her uncomfortable. 'Can I help in any way with the party? It seems like quite an ambitious undertaking for a bachelor.'

'Oh, I have lots of help. My housekeeper, Mrs Bates, is a frustrated army sergeant, and loves managing these affairs.'

'All right, then, if you're sure. I can come a little early if you like, to help with any last-minute preparations. Say, seven-thirty?'

'Wonderful. Come at noon if you like, then we could spend the day together.'

'Seven-thirty, Charles,' she said firmly. 'See you then.'

At six o'clock on the night of Charles's party, Lelia stood at her wardrobe trying to decide what to wear. She had cleared out most of her old designer wardrobe as unsuitable for her new lifestyle and now she couldn't make up her mind which of the four or five dresses hanging there would do for the occasion.

She didn't want to wear the same white dress she'd worn to dinner last Saturday, much as she liked it. There were two dresses, one black, one deep red, that were really too heavy for summer wear.

That left a pale yellow that she had to agree now did nothing for her complexion, and her old ashes of roses dress cut in the Grecian style that was really too low in front.

It was getting late, almost six-thirty. She'd have to decide. She put on the yellow dress and frowned at her reflection in the mirror. Her colour had improved in the last few months and with a little blusher and a light lipstick it might do.

She slipped it off and put on the pale rose. The colour was much better, she thought, but it dipped down a little too far in the neckline for comfort.

The telephone rang, and when she answered it on the bedroom extension, she heard Michael Fielding's deep voice.

'Lelia? It's Michael. I just spoke to Charles, and he suggested I pick you up and take you out to his place this evening.'

Lelia's skin prickled with annoyance. She wished Charles would quit treating her like a fragile piece of china.

'I see,' she said in a cold voice. Really, Charles was too much. And it put Michael on a spot, too. She'd only be an unwelcome intrusion on him and the lovely Karen. 'That really won't be necessary. I'd planned to drive myself.'

There was a short silence. 'As you please, he said. Then in a clipped tone, 'But it doesn't make sense to take two cars out there when we're both coming from the same direction. Charles didn't like the idea of your driving home alone late at night. Nor did I,' he added, 'especially when I'm only a few blocks away.'

She hesitated. Perhaps she was being too stubborn about her independence. She wanted to ask him if Karen wouldn't object to taking along a third party, but didn't like to appear to pry into his personal life.

His low voice broke the silence. 'If you're worried I'll try to force myself on you again,' he said curtly, 'you needn't.'

'Oh, no,' she broke in hurriedly, 'it's not that at all. It's just that Charles fusses so. And,' she added, 'I don't like to intrude.'

'Intrude on what?' he shot back. 'I don't understand.'

'Well,' she hedged, 'I thought—that is, I assumed. . .' She broke off, glad he wasn't there to see the flush that stole over her face. 'Won't you and Karen. . .?' she ended up lamely.

'Karen?' he asked. 'Karen's gone. She left this morning for Houston.'

'I see. Well, in that case, I suppose it does make sense not to take two cars.' She laughed. 'And it'll keep Charles happy.

'That's important to you?' he asked easily. 'To keep Charles happy?'

'Charles has been a good friend,' she replied slowly.

He didn't speak for a moment, and when he did his voice was brisk. 'Well, that's settled, then. Can you be ready in half an hour?'

'Yes, of course.'

When they hung up she stood staring down at the phone for a few minutes. So Karen was gone, she thought, and wondered what that meant.

*   *   *

'Charles tells me you've been working with retarded children,' Michael said later as they drove out along Gentilly Road to the lake. 'That sounds like quite a challenge.'

She turned to him eagerly. 'Oh, it is. But so satisfying.'

For some reason, she felt more at ease with him tonight than she ever had before, less threatened. She recalled how kind he had always been to her in the past, and except for that one episode a few weeks after Armand's death, how considerate of her feelings.

No longer overwhelmed by his mere presence, she could also appreciate his attractiveness in a more objective manner. Looking at him now as she recounted certain episodes at the children's centre that had especially touched her, she realised she could acknowledge his good looks, his closeness to her in the car, the way he smiled at her, without the fear that he was making an emotional demand on her. Even the dazzling blue eyes, which flashed away from the road in her direction from time to time, seemed now to be simply especially beautiful eyes, and she no longer felt they were probing dangerously into her very being.

'Well, here we are,' he said, pulling into the driveway of Charles's lakefront home. He shut off the engine and turned to her. 'I neglected to tell you how lovely you look tonight, Lelia. I especially like you in that dress.'

Lelia lowered her eyes. After his telephone call earlier, she hadn't had time to resume her inner debate over what to wear and had simply left on the pale rose dress. The low neckline still bothered her, but she had wrapped a lacy white stole around her shoulders for protection.

'Thank you,' she murmured. 'You cut a rather dashing figure yourself.'

It was true. His dark blue suit was beautifully cut and hung on his lean frame in a perfect fit. He had on a white dress shirt and a lighter blue tie that just matched the colour of his eyes.

He smiled faintly, nodded, then got out of the car and came around to her side. She noticed once again how gracefully he moved for such a tall man, like a born athlete. As he bent down to take her elbow, she glanced at him. His expression was composed, almost severe, his eyes half shut, the black eyelashes long and thick on his tanned high cheekbones; and when he touched her, a tremor went through her arm, even though the warm hand was light and impersonal.

They walked together down the steep steps that led to the street entrance of the house. From inside came the sounds of loud music, laughter, voices shouting to be heard.

Even though it was not yet eight o'clock, it sounded as though the party had got off to a roaring start. Suddenly, Lelia's heart constricted, and a sharp pang of anxiety spread through her.

This would be the first real party she had attended without the protection of a husband, a family, a distinct position in the New Orleans social hierarchy. Tonight she was here merely as herself, Lelia Duval, and not as part of an established contingent.

Her fingers tightened on her beaded bag, and her slim body swayed slightly. She closed her eyes, suddenly light-headed. Then she felt Michael's strong hand grasp her elbow firmly.

She glanced up at him. The blue eyes were hooded, the smile on the firm mouth gently mocking, but still kind.

'A touch of stage fright?' he murmured.

She nodded, blinked her eyes, then swallowed, her throat dry, and gave him a weak smile. 'A little,' she admitted.

His hand increased its pressure on her arm. 'It'll be OK,' he said with firm conviction. 'You'll be fine.'

The door opened then, increasing the noise from within by several decibels, and a beaming Charles appeared. Beyond him, the room seemed to be jammed with people. Lelia shrank back at the sights and sounds of the noisy crowd, and once again Michael's grip on her arm tightened, propelling her gently forward.

She took a gulp of air and stepped inside.

CHAPTER EIGHT

'HAPPY birthday, Charles,' Lelia raised her head and kissed him lightly on the cheek.

'Lelia. Michael,' Charles said delightedly. 'So good to see you.' The two men shook hands, and Charles put an arm around Lelia's waist, drawing her along with him. 'Come inside.'

The living room was very large and furnished in a stark modern style, with sleek blond furniture, the chairs upholstered in neutral earth tones. One whole wall was made of glass, looking out on a sweeping view of Lake Pontchartrain. It was an enormous lake, almost an inland sea, that stretched for miles across so that the far side was not even visible.

Charles's house faced north, and the sun was now quite low in the western sky, casting a golden swathe over the gently rippling blue water.

As Charles guided her forward into the crowd, Lelia looked around to see if Michael was still behind her. His hand had left her arm when Charles had clasped her waist so possessively.

He was gone, and she felt suddenly bereft in spite of Charles's reassuring presence. Glancing around the room, she caught sight of him standing tall and impressive in a group of people, a drink already in his hand.

With a sharp prick of annoyance she didn't understand, Lelia noticed that five out of the eight or so people in the group were women. One of them, a dark-haired beauty Charles used to squire around town, was gazing up at him with obvious interest. She saw him smile down at each one in turn, and although he seemed to be enjoying the admiring glances, his expression was inscrutable, the dazzling eyes giving away nothing of his inner thoughts.

Still, Lelia was annoyed. Why had he deserted her? Then, before she could look away, their eyes met across the room. Her irritation must have show on her face, because his eyes widened and he shrugged lightly, imperceptibly.

Recovering herself, she gave him a cool, polite smile and turned to Charles, who was handing her a drink and introducing her to a group of people standing around the bar.

'So this is the lovely Lelia Duval,' said a tall blond man. 'Where have you been hiding her, Charles?'

Lelia didn't know what to say, and only smiled, murmuring a faint 'How do you do' to him.

Charles laughed, and his arm tightened around her waist. 'This is Andy Stocker, Lelia, a fellow lawyer and as slippery and smooth as they come. Watch out for him.'

Andy Stocker was a striking-looking man, Lelia thought, and she wasn't sure how to react to him. He was almost as tall as Michael, deeply tanned and athletic-looking. His bright gold hair was cleverly styled, his greyish-blue eyes alight with pleasure, and as he smiled down at her, two deep dimples cut into his smooth cheeks.

'I'll be very careful,' she said, sipping her drink.

The doorbell rang again. Charles gave her a rueful

smile and released his hold on her. 'Excuse me, I'll be right back,' he said, and left them to greet his guests.

Andy Stocker immediately stepped to her side. She took another quick swallow of her drink. It tasted like it was only orange juice, but from the effect it had on her, she knew it must contain alcohol. She began to relax and listen to Andy's casual, entertaining chatter.

'I know I've seen you somewhere before,' he was saying earnestly, leaning towards her.

Lelia laughed. Even she wasn't that green. 'Oh, I'm sure you have,' she replied in a teasing tone. 'Me and every other woman in the room.'

He put on a hurt look and glanced at her empty glass. 'Here,' he said, 'you need another drink.'

'I don't know,' she said dubiously. She wasn't used to drinking. In spite of the very active social life she had led with Armand, Blanche always took care of supplying the drinks for their parties, and Lelia only drank wine as a rule. She looked at the glass Andy held out to her. 'What's in it?'

'Mostly orange juice. And just a little vodka,' he said, handing her the glass. 'It's called a screw-driver.'

She sipped cautiously. It *tasted* all right. Did that mean it was weak? Andy had his hand on her arm now. She didn't want to be rude to one of Charles's friends, but his closeness made her nervous. The drink seemed to give her confidence, and she took another long swallow.

'Shall we dance?' Andy started to lead her out onto the wide wooden verandah.

Lelia didn't know what to do. She looked around the room for a familiar face, but these people were all strangers to her. Although Charles had attended many of the Duval family's social functions in the past, they hadn't really travelled in the same circles.

There was no sign of either Charles or Michael. She glanced at Andy. At least she knew him. He was looking at her intently, his blond head cocked a little to one side, the light eyes appraising, assessing her somehow.

'Drink up,' he said in a low voice, 'and we'll dance.'

She swallowed the last of her drink, set the glass down on the bar and allowed Andy to lead her out onto the verandah. The sun had just gone down and it was getting dark.

There were several other couples on the dance floor. Someone had lit the Japanese lanterns strung across the balcony railing, and with the lake in the background, the music drifting out, it made a romantic setting.

When Andy turned to her and took her in his arms, she stumbled a little, and he held her tightly. She looked up at him with an apologetic smile, and was distressed to see that the outline of his head and shoulders had become distinctly fuzzy. She shook her head to clear it and blinked, but it didn't seem to help.

As they danced, she decided she'd be better off just closing his eyes, but that made the dizziness worse. Actually, she thought, it wasn't an unpleasant feeling. She worried a little about tripping again, but Andy was holding her so tightly that she didn't see how she could possibly fall.

Then she heard Charles calling to her. 'Lelia, there you are. I've been looking all over for you.'

She opened her eyes and focused them on Charles. He was threading his way through the couples on the dance floor towards her. Out in the fresh air, the worst of the dizziness seemed to have passed, and even in the dim light she could clearly see that his mouth was set in an angry line.

Andy loosened his hold on her and stepped back a pace. Charles took her by the arm and gave the blond man a swift glance.

'I can't have you monopolising Lelia,' he said evenly. 'I want her to meet my other guests.'

Charles began leading her away. She still felt a little light-headed, but with the passing of the dizziness, her old anxiety began to return. There were so many people here, and she didn't know any of them.

She did catch sight of Michael as they moved into the house. He was dancing with the dark girl who had been hanging on to his arm earlier. They were in a far corner of the verandah, and in the dim light of the coloured lanterns, she could just make out the grave expression on his face as he bent his head to listen to her.

Then Charles led her around the living room introducing her to everyone. Soon the sea of faces started to swim before her eyes. The muscles in her face began to ache painfully from her forced smile, and when someone handed her another drink, she sipped it gratefully. Once again, it seemed to take the edge off her nervousness.

'Charles, you haven't danced with me yet.' A tall redhead in an emerald-green dress was bearing down on them, and when she grasped his arm and started tugging at him, he turned to Lelia with an apologetic look.

'Don't worry about me, Charles. You have other guests. I'll be fine.'

When she was alone, she glanced around the crowded room, sipping her drink nervously. Everyone else seemed to be well-acquainted, and she felt out of place. She wondered how soon she could decently leave.

Then Andy Stocker was at her side. 'I see your watchdog has left you unprotected.' He grinned mischievously and held out his hand for her half-empty glass. 'Shall we dance, or are you Donaldson's exclusive property?'

Lelia bristled. The last drink had renewed her courage. 'I'm no one's property,' she said firmly.

'That's very good news,' Andy murmured. He held out his arms. 'Shall we?'

'Why not?' She quickly finished the rest of her drink and handed him her glass.

He set it down on a table, and soon they were back outside on the verandah, dancing again. It took Lelia only a few minutes of movement to realise that she had drunk far too much. Part of her was alarmed, but part of her didn't care.

Andy was holding her too tightly, she realised, but she was at the point where she was more than a little grateful for the support, since she wasn't absolutely sure of her own footing by now.

Somehow, her lacy stole had come off, and Andy's smooth warm hands were moving over her bare back, slowly and sensuously. His cheek was pressed against hers, and he was speaking in her ear, his warm breath gentle and seductive.

'Where do you live, Lelia? I'd like to see you again.'

'I live in the Vieux Carré. On Chartres Street.' Her eyes were closed again.

His hand slid up her back now to clasp the nape of her neck under the fall of thick dark hair. 'Will you have dinner with me one night next week?'

She opened her eyes. Everything seemed to be whirling around her. 'What night?' she murmured. She couldn't seem to concentrate.

'Any night you please, lady,' he breathed in a fervent tone.

Suddenly, the dizziness began to feel decidedly unpleasant. The glow that had been masking her nervousness turned to a gnawing feeling in her stomach. She hadn't had time for dinner before she left home, intending to eat something at the party.

The gnawing feeling gradually turned to a faint nausea. Horrified, she wondered if she was going to be sick. They were standing now in a far corner of the verandah. She put out a hand to grasp the railing and bent her head.

When she looked up at him, he was grinning wickedly down at her. 'Had a little too much to drink?'

'I. . .I. . .' she stammered and couldn't go on. It was suddenly overwhelmingly borne in on her just what a figure she must be cutting. She had just enough sense left to be deeply ashamed of what she'd done. The alcohol that she thought was a support to her nerves had betrayed her.

Her one thought was to get away before she disgraced herself completely. She was just able to focus her thoughts and gather herself together enough to smile at Andy.

'No, not really,' she forced out. 'But if you'll excuse me, I'd like to visit the powder room.'

'Hurry back,' he said in a low tone. He leaned over and kissed her lightly on the forehead.

She turned and with all her attention focused on walking a straight light, made her way into the house. She prayed she wouldn't see Michael or Charles. She'd find a telephone and call a taxi and get out of here as fast as she possibly could.

Somehow she managed to get through the crowd of people into a long hallway leading to the back of the house. After a tentative exploration behind two closed doors, she found Charles's bedroom and the phone extension on the bedside table. She sat down on the bed and fumbled with the phone book. The nausea was getting worse, and at last the moment came when she knew she couldn't fight it any longer.

She dropped the telephone book and just had time to make it into the adjoining bathroom, slam and lock the door behind her and lean over the basin before she was wretchedly, agonisingly sick.

When it was over, she felt terribly shaky, but the nausea was gone. She rinsed out her mouth with some mouthwash she found on the counter, and ran a comb through her hair. Now, she thought, I'll call the taxi and get home to bed. Every ounce of strength seemed to be drained out of her.

She opened the bathroom door and drew in her breath sharply when she saw Michael standing there staring at her, his arms folded across his chest, the blue eyes stern. When he took in her wretched state, however, the blue gaze softened. He took a step towards her.

'I was worried about you. Are you all right?'

She managed a weak smile. 'No, I'm not.' She hung her head. 'Please go,' she whispered. 'I'm going to call a taxi and go home.'

'Nonsense. I'll take you home.

Her eyes darted at him. 'Oh, no. There's no reason for you to leave the party.'

'I brought you,' he said flatly, 'and I'll take you home.'

She was too weak to protest. Tears stung her eyes. 'Michael,' she whispered, 'I'm so ashamed.'

In a second, he was before her. She slumped against him, weeping quietly, and his arms came around her, holding her gently, stroking her hair back from her forehead.

'Hey, now,' he murmured, 'there's no reason on earth for you to feel that way. It has to happen to everyone once.' He drew away from her and put a hand under her chin, tilting her face up. She had stopped crying, but her face was wet and her eyes still glistened.

She felt his thumbs moving across her cheeks, wiping the tears. As she gazed up at him, she remembered the day at Beaux Champs, the day she saw the deer. He had comforted her then in the same way he was now.

She remembered, too, what had happened afterwards, and she wondered if he would kiss her again. She wanted him to, she realised with a little shock. Her eyes were fixed now on that firm mouth, sensitive and gentle in spite of its hard lines. She wanted to feel it pressing against hers, wanted those arms to hold her again, wanted to feel the tautly muscled length of that tall body against hers.

There was a tense silence in the room. They stood motionless, as if paralysed in a static tableau. His hands had stopped moving on her cheeks and were placed on either side of her head. She couldn't take her eyes from his mouth, and she knew he was well aware of her fixed gaze. She wondered if he was equally well aware of the thudding of her heart, the warm glow that had begun to course through her.

His hands slid down to her neck, then, and she shivered a little with pleasure at his touch on her skin. As his head made a slight motion towards her, she felt her lips soften and part of their own volition in anticipation of his kiss.

Then, suddenly, his hands left her. He drew back, his face a mask. He smiled with an obvious effort, ruefully, and sighed.

'I'd better get you home,' he said lightly.

Lelia couldn't have felt worse if he'd slapped her across the face. A chill ran through her. He must know, she thought, just how eager I was, and her cheeks burned.

'Are you sure. . . ?' She thought of the dark woman he'd been dancing with. Perhaps she was the reason he didn't want to kiss her.

'I'm sure,' he said. He turned and started walking towards the door.

'But if there's someone waiting for you. . .' she faltered.

He whirled around and gave her a hard stare as though trying to read her thoughts. 'No one important,' he said. He held out a hand. 'Let's go.'

Lelia fell asleep on the drive home and didn't wake up until she felt the car come to a stop. Opening her eyes, she realised they were in front of her house. She also realised that her head was resting on a hard muscled shoulder and that a strong arm was around her, holding her close.

She closed her eyes again and didn't move. Somehow, she didn't want the moment to end. It was very quiet. She could hear Michael's steady breathing, feel the rough texture of his jacket on the skin of her cheek and bare shoulders, his warm hand solidly grasping her forearm. Her face was turned into his neck, and, opening her eyes, she saw that by moving just an inch or two closer, her lips would rest on that long, strong column.

She looked up at him sleepily, and the blue eyes gazed down at her. His fingers moved very slightly on her arm, and she could feel his breath quicken. A warmth started to spread through her, and her pulse began to race.

Then he smiled. 'Feeling better?' He removed his arm.

She lowered her eyes and moved away from him, hurt at his withdrawal. She felt cold and suddenly very alone.

'Yes, much better.' She looked at him. 'Michael, I'm so sorry.' She bit her lip. 'I've ruined the party for you and disgraced myself. I didn't even thank Charles or say goodnight.'

'Don't worry about me. I was ready to leave anyway. You gave me a good excuse. And Charles will understand.' His voice hardened. 'He should have known better than to leave you in the hands of a fast operator like Andy Stocker in the first place.'

'Oh, you're wrong about Andy,' she protested. 'He was very kind. It wasn't his fault. He did nothing wrong.'

Michael merely raised an eyebrow and shrugged. Then, 'Sorry,' he said, 'I once got the impression that you weren't interested in that kind of thing.' He laughed shortly. 'I must have misunderstood. You don't mind Stocker pawing you, only me.'

'He wasn't pawing,' she objected heatedly.

Michael only frowned. 'Pardon me,' he said in an icy tone, 'but it looked that way to me. His hands were all over you.'

Lelia began to grow angry. She dimly sensed that Michael's consistent rejection of her tonight, the way he deliberately ignored the opportunities to kiss her, was at the bottom of her annoyance. Now, to have him accuse her of allowing Andy Stocker liberties he himself didn't choose to take, seemed irrational.

'I'm surprised you noticed,' she snapped at him. 'You were so busy with that dark-haired woman. Just your type, isn't she?'

He gave her a long appraising look, then a slow smile spread across his face. He leaned back against the car door, a strange light of satisfaction in his eyes. Then he sobered.

'I told you once, Lelia,' he said softly. 'You're my type.'

At his words, her heart gave a joyful leap. She wanted to ask him why, then, he had backed off when she had been so ready to welcome his kiss. But she knew she could do no such thing. She sighed and turned her head.

'I'd better go in now,' she said. 'I'm sorry I was rude a minute ago. It's been a bad night.'

Still gazing at her intently, he opened his mouth as if to speak, apparently thought better of it, and set his lips in a firm line. Nodding shortly, he said, 'Yes. Of course.'

As they walked to her front door, she wondered if she should invite him in. Better not, she thought. She had already revealed too much to him tonight, and she found now she wanted only the safety of her own home. She wasn't ready yet to handle all these erotic undercurrents. Perhaps she never would be.

She unlocked the door and turned to him. 'Thank you again, Michael. I really appreciate the way you came to my rescue tonight, and I do apologise for behaving so badly.'

He shrugged. 'Not at all. You learned something, I'm sure.'

'I certainly did,' she said fervently, making a face. 'No more vodka for me.'

He laughed easily and put a hand lightly on her cheek. 'Good girl.' He hesitated, looking down at her intently for a moment, then said, 'Goodnight, Lelia.'

Abruptly, he turned from her and walked down the path to the car. Lelia stepped inside and locked the door behind her. As she walked down the hall to her bedroom, she tried to sort out the events of the disturbing evening, to make some sense of her feelings.

She had to admit to herself that she had been very attracted to Michael and had felt secure and comfortable with him when he took her home. But, then, she had been in a weakened condition and grateful for a familiar face to turn to in her distress.

Later, lying in bed, she realised she was glad now he hadn't kissed her. Had he known how vulnerable she was? Could that have been why he didn't take advantage of the situation? Or was he no longer interested in her?

She thought about the beautiful Karen Swenson and wondered again just what their relationship was. It was close, of that she was sure, but how close?

She finally managed to quiet the turmoil of her

thoughts by telling herself firmly that she had been right in the first place to put up a barrier against the disturbing Michael Fielding. It would be too easy to fall into a relationship with him where she could get terribly hurt, too easy to make a fool of herself, too easy to fall in love with him.

CHAPTER NINE

LELIA slept late the next morning and barely made it to the eleven o'clock Mass at St Louis. When she first awakened, with a dry mouth and pounding head, she realised ruefully that she had a hangover, but after orange juice, strong coffee, and the brisk walk to and from the Basilica, she felt almost human again.

When she arrived back at Chartres Street, the long Sunday afternoon stretched emptily ahead of her, and she decided she wanted some company. On an impulse, she called Madame and invited her down to lunch. The work on the house was virtually complete, and she didn't go to the centre on Sundays.

They ate out in the courtyard. It was blistering hot already, but there was some shade here, and both women detested air-conditioning. Lelia had changed into brief shorts and a halter top and pinned her hair up loosely on top of her head.

'You like music, don't you, Lelia?' Madame asked as they ate. Lelia had fixed a seafood salad, crusty rolls and iced tea.

'Very much.'

'I wonder, then,' Madame went on in a diffident manner, 'if you would be at all interested in attending a recital later this afternoon of one of my pupils. It's Bianca Felstad, a very gifted contralto.'

Lelia knew the name, a young singer who had begun to

make a name for herself at the New York City Opera and was to make her début at the Met in the fall.

'I'd love to,' she replied immedtely, her dark eyes alight with pleasure. 'Thank you very much.'

'Not at all. You've been very kind to me.' She laughed. 'A most agreeable landlady.' Pausing, she chewed thoughtfully for a moment, then went on. 'I believe our arrangement is working out satisfactorily. I know it is for me. It's been over a month now.'

'So it has,' Lelia said, taken by surprise. 'The time has gone by so fast.' She smiled warmly at Madame. 'Yes, it's a wonderful arrangement. I'm quite happy with it.'

Madame smiled with satisfaction. 'That's all right, then.'

The telephone extension on the patio rang shrilly. 'Excuse me,' Lelia said and crossed over to a small table by the door to answer it.

It was Charles, wondering what had happened to her last night.

'Oh, Charles, I was going to call you later to apologise for leaving so suddenly without even saying goodbye.'

'I was worried about you.' There was a note of petulance in his voice.

'I'm so sorry. I just suddenly felt quite ill. I was going to call a cab, but Michael showed up and insisted on driving me home.'

He was immediately contrite. 'That's all right, then. Andy Stocker disappeared just after you did, and I put two and two together. . .'

'And got five,' Lelia broke in, half-amused, half-annoyed. Charles was a good friend, but he had no right to spy on her.

'Something like that,' he admitted. He paused. 'Andy seemed to be quite taken with you. Are you going to see him again?'

She was really annoyed now, but managed to laugh lightly. 'I don't know. He hasn't asked me.'

'Watch out for him, Lelia.' he warned solemnly. 'He's got quite a reputation.'

'I can look after myself, Charles.' After her performance last night, she knew this wasn't quite true, but, then, she believed she had learned her lesson. 'Madame Fiorini and I are having lunch, Charles. I've got to go.'

Her cheeks were burning when she went back to the wrought-iron table. Madame only gave her a quick look, blinking twice, and sipped her iced tea.

'Mr Donaldson is very protective of you,' she remarked at last.

'Yes,' Lelia agreed with a dry smile, 'a little too much so.'

Madame nodded. She broke and buttered a roll slowly. 'Yet, such a friend is valuable.' She smiled. 'I think, though, he would prefer a closer tie with you than friendship.'

Lelia opened her mouth to reply, but the telephone shrilled again. She shrugged apologetically and ran to answer it.

'Lelia?' came a strange masculine voice. 'Lelia Duval?'

'Yes,' she said cautiously. The voice was vaguely familiar.

'It's Andy,' he said in a confident tone. 'Andy Stocker. I just called to see how you were. You vanished into thin air last night, before I could even say goodnight.'

'Oh,' she said weakly, reddening. 'Yes, Andy. I—I'm

fine.' She wasn't. She was mortified.

He chuckled. 'You were really green around the gills last night,' came the cheerful voice. 'Not to worry, sweetheart. It happens to the best of us at least once.'

Somehow her breezy manner made her feel better. 'Once is more than enough for me, thank you,' she said drily.

He laughed at that. 'I thought you were new at the game.' His voice lowered confidentially. 'Listen, Lelia, the reason I called is that I'd like to see you again. How about dinner some night? Friday? Saturday?' When she didn't answer, he rushed on. 'Monday. Tuesday. Wednesday. . .'

'Stop it,' she said, laughing in spite of her trepidation. She hesitated a few minutes, then said, 'Andy, I'm not sure.' She wanted to be honest with him.

'Listen, Charles told me you were widowed recently. I'll back off for a while if you're not ready. Say, a week?'

She could imagine the broad grin on his face, 'Say, a month,' she replied firmly. 'At least.'

They said goodbye, then, and Lelia walked back to Madame, an amused smile still playing about her lips. Madame was gazing at her, eyebrows lifted.

'Your social life seems to be picking up quite dramatically,' she commented casually.

Lelia spread her hands and shrugged. 'A little more than I'm equipped to deal with, I'm afraid.' She frowned. 'I'm just not used to. . .to. . .'

'To being sought out by men?' Madame finished up for her on a dry note. She shifted in her chair. 'I can see that. It's all right. Take your time. You are under no obligation to do everything others want you to do. We all have to learn that we really do have the right to say no.'

Lelia shot her a grateful look. 'You do understand,' she murmured.

'Oh, yes. I understand quite well. For example, I understand that neither of these men who seek your company—how does the phrase go?—turn you on? A little crude, but apt. Am I right?'

Lelia nodded, embarrassed. It was true. She liked Charles and Andy, but could live without them.

'Now, I've annoyed you,' Madame said with a frown. 'I'm sorry. Usually I never pry. You just seem so—so innocent, somehow, vulnerable, even though you've been married.'

'Oh, no, Madame. You're not prying. I appreciate your interest. I've never really had anyone to confide in, and I don't know much about friendship.'

'Well, Lelia, I'm not asking you to confide in me, but I am your friend.'

'I know,' Lelia said, 'and I appreciate it.' She started stacking dishes on a tray. 'I have a lemon sorbet for dessert. Would you like coffee?'

'Yes, please.' She took out a packet of cigarettes. 'Do you mind?'

Lelia shook her head. 'Of course not. But I thought singers never smoked.'

Madame lit a cigarette and smiled. 'One of the compensations of retirement, my dear.'

While Lelia was in the kitchen waiting for the coffee to drip, the doorbell rang. It was Michael, and the minute she saw him, tall and handsome in a pair of tan cord trousers and dark brown knit shirt, her heart skipped a beat, then settled into a pounding rhythm in her ears.

'Michael,' she said, looking into those dazzling blue eyes.

'I just stopped by to see how you were.' His tone was casual, almost distant, but there was genuine concern in his voice.

'I'm fine,' she faltered, then hesitated, not sure what to do. Finally, she decided that she was being silly. He was making a kind gesture, nothing more. It was time to stop being so edgy around him. If he had ever been romantically interested in her, he certainly wasn't any longer. She opened the door wider. 'Won't you come in?'

He nodded and stepped inside. Alone now in the cool dim foyer, it suddenly dawned on her that she was only wearing those brief shorts and a halter. Was that the reason for the brooding gaze he was giving her?

She turned and started towards the kitchen calling to him over her shoulder as he followed. 'Madame Fiorini and I just had lunch. I've made some coffee. Would you like a cup?'

They were in the kitchen now. 'Please,' he said, 'I'll carry the tray.'

Out in the courtyard, she introduced Michael to Madame. 'My tenant,' she added. When they sat down at the table, she said to her, 'Michael bought the house on Dauphine Street I think you may have wanted. He's a restoration architect. He did all the work at the Duval family plantation, Beaux Champs, and has worked all over the world.'

She knew she was babbling and bit her lower lip in confusion. Her hands shook slightly as she poured the coffee, and she prayed the others wouldn't notice.

'You sound like a press agent, Lelia,' Michael said,

taking a cup from her. 'Actually, the main reason I stopped by is to see if you'd care to come and see what I'm doing with the house.' He turned to Madame. 'And you, too, Madame Fiorini, since you were interested in it yourself.'

'Oh, I'm sorry, I can't today, Michael,' Lelia said in a rush. She wished this man didn't *unnerve* her so. 'Madame is taking me to a recital.'

He nodded. 'Some other time, then.'

Madame's dark eyes flashed knowingly from one to the other. She took a swallow of coffee. 'So, Mr Fielding, you were the one who bought the house I had my eye on. Tell me, do you plan to live there when your work is finished, or may I hope that it will be on the market again one day? If so, I'd like to have first refusal.'

'I haven't decided yet,' Michael answered. He flicked a glance at Lelia and set his cup down carefully in its saucer. 'That depends.' His tone was unreadable.

While he and Madame discussed the Dauphine Street house, Lelia sat silently, half-listening to the technical discussion, half-mulling over his last comment. Depends on what? she wondered. Karen?

Finally, Michael drained the last of his coffee and stood up. 'Thank you for the coffee, Lelia. And the conversation. It was nice to meet you, Madame Fiorini. Perhaps we'll meet again.'

Madame nodded her head slightly and smiled. When Lelia started to rise, Michael put a hand out. 'Don't bother to see me out. I know the way.'

With that he was gone. Lelia started collecting the cups and saucers, aware of Madame's piercing eyes on her all the while.

'A very pleasant man,' she said casually at last. 'Very handsome, too.'

'Yes,' Lelia murmured absently. 'I guess he is.'

Madame got up to go. 'He's different from the other two.'

Lelia gave her a sharp look. 'The other two?'

Madame smiled. 'The two men who called earlier.' She waved a hand, sparkling with rings. 'With them, you were quite collected, cool, sure of yourself. I sensed that Mr Fielding made you slightly nervous. I just wondered why.'

Lelia shrugged, thinking it over. 'I don't know why,' she answered truthfully. 'Once, I thought. . .' She broke off, unwilling to go into the past. She shrugged again. 'There's really no reason. He's been very kind to me.'

It was true, she thought. Suddenly she wished she had been able to go with him to his house this afternoon. When he asked her, she had been glad she had an excuse not to go. Now she wasn't so sure.

During the next week, Lelia found her thoughts turning often to Michael Fielding, trying to understand his motivation and her own feelings.

If he wasn't interested in her any more, as she had begun to suspect, why did he want to see her? And if she was grateful that he left her alone, why did she find him so often on her mind, to the point where she jumped every time the phone rang?

Finally, he did call her, just when she had decided he wasn't going to ever again. She was so glad to hear from him at last that she agreed immediately when he asked her out to dinner with him the following Saturday night.

Unlike Charles, he didn't ask her where she wanted to

go, and when he showed up at her doorstep that Saturday night, tall and handsome in a dark suit, she didn't see the sleek Peugeot at the kerb.

'You're all ready,' he remarked approvingly. 'I thought we'd have dinner at the Court of the Two Sisters. We can walk.' He smiled down at her with obvious pleasure.

She had bought a new dress for the occasion, a soft silk tissue faille in a wonderful shade of deep cherry red that did marvels for her creamy complexion and dark hair. The neckline was low and square with wide bands over the shoulders.

At the restaurant, they sat outside under the magnolia trees. There were candles on the tables to keep the flying insects at bay and soft mushroom lights scattered about the spacious lawns. A fountain in the centre of the court splashed gently into a concrete pool.

'What would you like to drink?' Michael asked when the waitress appeared. He raised a dark brow at her and a smile flicked briefly over his solemn face.

Lelia flushed and lowered her eyes. 'I'll have a glass of cream sherry,' she replied firmly. She glanced across the table at him. Their eyes met and she had to smile at his gently mocking expression. 'I've learned my lesson.'

He was leaning forward, elbows on the table, his hands laced together under his chin. He nodded at her gravely and gave their order to the waitress.

'I'm sorry I couldn't come with you last Sunday to see your house,' Lelia said.

He shrugged. 'There's plenty of time. Actually, it's just in the first stages anyway. How was the recital?'

As they chatted over their drinks and later through

dinner, Lelia began to wonder why she had ever been afraid of him. He was easy to be with, and although she was well aware of the occasional appreciative glances he cast her way from time to time, she felt somehow safe and secure with him.

'You've managed quite well on your own, haven't you, Lelia?' he asked over coffee. He lit a cigarette and leaned back in his chair. 'Done all the things you set out to do, proved you could manage on your own.'

'I think I've made a good start,' she said carefully. 'At least I feel I'm being of some small use in the world.'

'Did your nuns teach you that?' he asked lightly. 'The importance of service?'

She frowned a little and sipped her coffee, thinking over his question. 'Partly,' she said slowly. 'They believed in service, of course, but not only for the sake of the person served. It's hard to explain.'

'I think I understand. "It's more blessed to give than to receive."'

Her eyes lit up. 'Exactly. Giving really is a joy. To be needed.' Her voice trailed off. 'I don't mean to sound sanctimonious.'

His hand shot across the table and covered hers. 'Not at all. I know the kind of person you are, the depth of your character.'

At that touch of his hand on hers, a little electric current seemed to run up her arm and spread warmly through her body. This disturbed her a little, but the sensation was decidedly pleasurable. She moved her own hand fractionally under his and his arm drew back.

He stood up. 'Shall we go? It's early yet. I thought we might get lucky and find a spot to sit at Preservation Hall.'

'I doubt that,' she said, rising to her feet. 'Not during the tourist season.'

They walked companionably along the crowded streets towards the historic hall where local and visiting jazz musicians gathered nightly for impromptu jam sessions. It was always crowded, but especially so in the summer.

A group of people brushed past them, laughing and talking loudly, brandishing the hurricane glass that were given out as souvenirs at several nightspots. Michael's arm came around her shoulders as one of them jostled her, and at the touch of his lightly calloused hand on her bare arm, Lelia experienced the same little shock she had at the dinner table.

He looked down at her with a wry smile. 'Tourists!' he said and made a face.

His hand slid down to clasp her around the waist, holding her to his long lithe body protectively. It was a casual, natural gesture from a man to a woman. There was nothing remotely suggestive about it, and Lelia leaned against him as he matched his stride to hers, grateful for his strength, the sheltering arm, among the crowds.

They did manage to squeeze on to one of the long hard wooden benches in Preservation Hall. The music was in full swing, typical New Orleans dixieland jazz, filling the small room with its happy throbbing jungle beat.

There was a booming, sliding trombone, two blaring trumpets, a clarinet that trilled and flew all over the scale, a frenetic drummer, and a bored black piano player with a cigarette dangling out of his mouth.

The hall was jammed. People were standing at the back and sides now, clapping and stamping their feet to the wild strains of 'South Rampart Street Parade' and 'Muskrat Ramble'.

Michael held her very tightly, protecting her from the swaying shouting crowd that surged around them, beside them, in back of them. At one point he leaned down to speak to her, but she couldn't hear him over the noise. She shrugged helplessly, and he put his face next to hers, his mouth at her ear.

'Are you OK?' he shouted.

Suddenly, all Lelia was conscious of was that rough cheek on her face, the warm breath in her ear, the tangy masculine scent of his skin. Her eyes widened at how the nearness of him made her feel. She could see the way his black hair curled very slightly at the back of his neck, the sparser hairs beneath on the tanned skin, the way his crisp white shirt collar bit into the side of his neck, and had a sudden impulse to reach out and touch him.

Then his hard cheek slid against hers as he drew back to look at her. She gazed up into the dazzling blue eyes, mesmerised by their brilliance, their faces not quite touching. Her throat felt dry, her face warm.

Finally, she smiled and nodded, mouthing the word 'Fine' so he would know she was all right. He smiled back at her, gave her shoulders a squeeze, then bent his head and kissed her lightly, briefly, on the mouth.

By the time they left, an hour later, Lelia was in a daze, both from the loud music and the closeness to Michael. She stumbled out of the hall ahead of him, his hands firmly on her shoulders, guiding her, protecting her, until they were back out on the street.

It was much cooler outside, and it was a relief to get out of the noisy smoke-filled room. Michael kept a light grip on her shoulders and turned her around to face him. He grinned down at her.

'That was quite an experience,' he said. She swayed slightly, and his hold on her tightened. 'Are you all right?'

She smiled and ran a hand over her dark hair. 'I think so. I'm just not used to crowds like that.'

He frowned. 'No. I know that. Maybe I shouldn't have taken you.'

'Oh, no, don't say that,' she protested. 'I wouldn't have missed it for the world. I've always wanted to go to Preservation Hall, but, of course, with Armand. . .' She shrugged.

'Of course,' he said curtly, and nodded.

They turned, then, and started walking towards Chartres Street, and when he took her hand, it seemed natural and right to her.

At her door, she took out her house key and turned to him, suddenly shy. She wanted to invite him inside, but was a little apprehensive about being alone with him. She could feel her pulse quicken as he reached over and took the key from her hand. He unlocked the door, pushed it open and handed her back the key.

'It was a lovely evening,' she said at last. 'Thank you, Michael.'

'Entirely my pleasure,' he said with a slight bow.

She looked up at him. From the light of the dim lamp at the side of the door, she could see the hooded eyes, the hard flat planes of his cheek. He seemed to be debating within himself.

Then he put one hand at her throat, the other at the back of her head and slowly bent his head down towards her. She closed her eyes, suddenly anxious. Her heart simply stopped for a second, then, as she felt the touch of his lips on hers, it started pounding again rapidly.

The kiss was gentle, almost chaste, but when she felt the pressure of his hand at the base of her throat increase, then slide downward so that his palm was flat against her bare upper chest, moving slowly back and forth, she drew in her breath sharply.

The dark head came up then, and his hands left her. 'Goodnight, then, Lelia,' he said, and turned to walk down the path.

She watched him for a moment, confused at his abrupt departure, then slipped inside the house and shut the door behind her. In the darkened drawing room, she went to the windows to draw the curtains shut, and she could see him still standing on the pavement at the front of the house. She watched as he lit a cigarette, the flame of the match briefly illuminating the clean lines of his profile. When she drew the curtain and switched on a light, she could hear his footsteps moving away down the street.

She went to her bedroom, then, and as she got ready for bed, her mood was pensive. She examined her feelings, trying to make sense of the conflict within her.

To be honest, she thought, as she slipped into bed, tonight had been the most pleasant evening she could remember having in years. Not only was Michael good company, but she liked him as a person. He made no demands on her, and she didn't have the feeling, as she had with Andy Stocker, that he would embroil her in sexual games she wasn't ready for. She trusted him.

Well, she thought, I trust Charles, too, but I don't

enjoy his company as much as I do Michael's. Lying on her back in the dark, she mulled this over. What was it about Michael that she found so compelling, while with Charles she merely felt a vague affection?

She thought then of Michael's touch on her arm, her throat, his cheek against hers, his soft breath in her ear. She thought of his kiss on the doorstep, the way it had made her feel.

Was that the difference? She tolerated Andy's flirtatiousness, Charles's mild pecks, but she had longed to feel Michael's mouth on hers. What was more, she admitted at last, she hadn't wanted him to go. She had enjoyed that brief kiss. Too brief, she thought now, and felt a rush of longing surge up in her that was close to a physical pain.

CHAPTER TEN

FOR THE next few weeks, Lelia saw Michael at least once a week, sometimes more, unless he was out of town. He would stop by late in the afternoon occasionally and they would sit together out in the courtyard over a glass of lemonade or a cup of coffee. On the weekends, they would go out to dinner or dancing or to a show, and Lelia finally worked up the courage to go inside one of the raucous Bourbon Street honkytonks.

Michael had laughed at her when they emerged out on the street after the show. Lelia's face was a sheet of flame. Her convent upbringing and sheltered marriage hadn't begun to prepare her for the near-nude strip show or the comedy routine full of salacious innuendo she didn't comprehend the half of.

'You asked for it,' he had taunted her, highly amused at her speechless embarrassment. 'It wasn't my idea.'

Finally, she had to laugh with him. He was right. She had suggested it, driven by curiosity, a desire to experience all of life, and besides, she was with Michael. Nothing bad could happen to her. She was safe with him.

During those carefree, happy weeks, she knew that Karen was in town occasionally. This troubled her, although the beautiful blonde girl's presence in New Orleans seemed to have no effect on Michael's attentiveness. She still wondered what their relationship was, but couldn't bring herself to ask outright.

Once or twice, when they were alone, driving in the car or dancing or seated side by side in a restaurant, she had almost brought the subject up. She always stopped herself, however. She didn't want to overstep any boundaries, boundaries, she realised, that Michael himself had set up. For while he was attentive, unfailingly courteous and considerate, and seemed to enjoy her company as much as she did his, their relationship had remained static.

This puzzled Lelia. She enjoyed his calm, mild kisses, his touch on her arm, around her shoulders, her waist, and couldn't help wondering why he always drew back from her, as if he arbitrarily set up an invisible line he would not cross.

When she was with him, close to him, when his lips brushed lightly on hers, she longed sometimes to throw her arms around his neck and pull him to her. On the other hand, when she was away from him, she was grateful for his restraint. But was it restraint? She wondered. Or was it lack of interest?

She knew from the past that he was an intensely virile, passionate man, that he was unused to celibacy, and that he was very attractive to women. Sometimes she almost wondered if she had dreamed that episode in her kitchen so long ago, right after Armand died.

She had rejected him then, firmly and decisively, sent him away. Into Karen's arms? she wondered. Yet, he had come back. He must like her, enjoy her company. If Karen was filling his physical needs, as she suspected, then that must be the reason he stayed at a distance from her.

One night in late September they were driving back to

Chartres Street from a party at Charles's house on the lake. It had been a casual affair, a barbecue, the last outdoor event of the summer, most likely. Soon the weather would turn cool, and even now Lelia shivered a little in her light halter top.

'Cold?' Michael asked. His arm came around her, pulling her close to him, and the warmth of his body stole through her as she nestled comfortably against him.

She smiled up at him, and the blue eyes flicked briefly down at her as his hold on her tightened.

They were touching now all along the length of their thighs. Michael had on a pair of lightweight trousers and a dark blue knit shirt. His arms were bare, the strong muscles rippling as he drove through the busy streets of the French Quarter. He removed his arm, and Lelia felt a sudden chill.

At her door, he took her key from her as always. He unlocked the door, handed the key back to her, and she turned to him for his brief kiss.

'I'd like to come in for a while tonight, if I may, Lelia,' he said in a low voice.

She widened her eyes at his grave tone, then smiled. 'Of course,' she said.

He followed her into the drawing room. She closed the curtains and switched on a lamp.

'Sit down, Michael. Would you like a drink?'

He crossed to a wide sofa and sat down, his eyes fastened on her. 'No. Not now,' he replied. His long legs were spread apart, his elbows resting on his knees. 'Come and sit down.'

She hesitated. Something in his tone frightened her. It was almost as though he had some bad news to break to her. Anxiety filled her heart. Was he going to leave? With Karen?

Slowly she walked over to the couch and sat beside him. She waited in breathless anticipation for him to speak. He turned to her.

'Lelia, we've been together quite a lot these past weeks,' he began. 'I've enjoyed seeing you, being with you.' He paused. 'I think—I hope—you've enjoyed it, too.'

'Oh, yes, Michael. Very much.' She sat quite still, her hands clasped in her lap. She steeled herself for what was coming and gave him a quick apprehensive glance.

'I've come to care for you very much,' he went on in a sombre tone. 'I hope you've begun to care a little for me.' Before she could answer, he ran an impatient hand through his thick black hair. 'Hell,' he muttered, 'I don't know how to go about this. I've never done it before.' He stared down into her eyes and said simply, 'I love you, Lelia. I'm asking you to marry me.'

Her eyes widened. 'Marry you!' she breathed in a shocked tone. She drew back. 'I can't marry you. It's impossible.'

He grabbed her by the shoulders and shook her a little. 'Well, what do you want, then?' he growled. 'Do you want me out of your life entirely? Because I'll tell you honestly, Lelia, married or not, I can't keep my hands off you any longer.'

He groaned aloud, and the next thing she knew his arms had come around her, crushing her to him. The dark head came down and his mouth covered hers in a searing, demanding kiss that broke down all the carefully erected barriers of the past weeks in a possession that literally took Lelia's breath away.

The cool mild kisses of before were forgotten in the tumultuous feelings this invasion aroused in her. Her lips parted under his, and when his probing tongue touched hers, a bright light seemed to go on inside her head, and an explosion of pounding blood began to race through her veins.

Mindless now, her defences shattered, she groped blindly for him and flung her arms around his neck. His hands moved feverishly on her bare back, down along her spine, slipping briefly under the waistband of her skirt, then back up along her ribcage, his thumbs brushing the sides of her breasts under the skimpy halter.

He tore his mouth from hers then, and she could feel his harsh breathing in her ear.

'Oh, God, Lelia, how I've wanted you. I've ached to have you in my arms like this. All these weeks. . .' His voice broke off, then, and he kissed her again, more deeply than before.

She responded to him totally, instinctively, meeting him all the way, breathless with passion, as though an enormous force bottled up inside her had suddenly been released.

He had one arm tightly around her neck, and now the other slid around to her throat, pushing her head back against the stack of pillows on the sofa. He leaned over her, and the hand moved down to cover her breast.

She gasped, clutching at him, as he began to unbutton the front of her halter. Her hands slipped up under his shirt, roamed freely over the strong muscles of his back and around to his smooth chest. She could feel his heart thundering under her fingers.

He pushed aside the halter and when his hand came down on her bare breast she arched her body towards him. She was lying down now, her head propped up on the pillows, her head flung back in an abandonment of ecstasy. Both his hands were on her breasts now, and his thumbs moved lightly over the taut nipples, bringing her to such a pitch of desire that she moaned deep in her throat.

Then, as his long sensitive fingers cupped underneath the rounded fullness, he brought his mouth down, kissing first one rosy peak, then the other. He was lying half on top of her now so that she was conscious of his need and desire.

His hands slid up to clasp her face on either side. She opened her eyes, drugged with passion, and gazed up at him, her lips apart. The blue gaze penetrated to her very soul.

'I love you, Lelia,' he choked out. 'I love you so much. Say you'll marry me. I want you to belong to me.'

A cold chill struck Lelia's heart at his words, dampening her ardour. Marry him! she thought. Belong to him! Never! She couldn't do that. Not again. She shuddered and turned her head away.

'Don't do that!' he rasped out, forcing her head back to face him. 'Don't leave me like that.'

She looked up at him with pleading eyes. 'I can't marry you, Michael. I can't marry anyone. I'd rather die than belong to anyone ever again.'

She could see that he was only controlling his anger with tremendous effort. 'Lelia, I am not Armand.' He bit out each word with bullet-like precision.

She cowered before his barely contained fury, but was

determined to be firm. 'No,' she agreed, her voice almost a whisper, 'but you're doing the same thing. You want the same thing. To own me.'

'That's not true!' he shouted. 'I don't want to own you, I only want to love you.' Then, when he saw the frightened look on her face, he groaned and turned his head away. 'I've tried to be patient with you, Lelia. I've kept my distance.' He looked at her. 'I wanted to give you a chance to get to know you, to trust me. And,' he added softly, 'to want me.'

She bit her lip and closed her eyes, unable to speak. Of course she wanted him. When his very touch made her tremble with longing and his kisses set her pulses racing with liquid fire. But belong to him? To anyone, ever again? It simply wasn't possible.

Slowly, he pulled her halter together and buttoned it. Even now, the touch of his hand as it moved lightly over her breast sent shafts of desire through her, but she steeled herself against it.

He sat up straight and pulled her gently up beside him. He forced her to look into his eyes.

'I'll ask once more, Lelia. Will you marry me?'

She turned away, unable to face him. 'I can't,' she whispered on a sob.

For a long moment he sat perfectly still beside her. Then she heard him sigh deeply, rise up in his chair and walk away from her. She sat rigid, unmoving, until she heard the front door close behind him and his steps fading away down the street.

Then she began to cry. 'Michael,' she groaned aloud through her tears. 'Oh, Michael.'

* * *

During the next few weeks, the pain of loss was so intense at times that Lelia was afraid she would break down completely. She had suffered in her marriage to Armand, but that was only a dull ache compared to the searing agony that welled up in her whenever she thought of Michael.

She knew he meant what he said. He had asked her for the last time to marry him that night, and she had refused. She would never see him again. She must put him out of her mind and heart.

In spite of the torment, she never once doubted she had been right to send him away. To risk a repetition of her marriage to Armand would be worse than a death sentence. The present pain would pass, she told herself. She would get over it. Only, it seemed to be taking such a long time!

One morning towards the end of October, Madame Fiorini invited her upstairs for coffee. They sat at the breakfast nook in the corner of the small kitchen overlooking the courtyard. The leaves were falling now. Soon it would be winter.

'If you don't mind a rather personal observation, Lelia,' Madame was saying, 'you aren't looking at all well lately.'

Lelia gave her a quick glance. She knew it was true. She only picked at her food and wasn't sleeping well. She forced out a smile. 'Perhaps I need a vacation.' She tried to make her voice light.

Madame gave her a cool appraising look over her coffee cup. 'Perhaps,' she murmured. There was a long silence. Lelia stared blankly out the window and drank her coffee.

'I haven't seen your charming Mr Fielding around for some time,' Madame said casually at last. 'Is he out of town?'

At the mention of his name, tears came to Lelia's eyes. She couldn't help it. She turned to Madame with a stricken look, the hot tears coursing unchecked down her face.

'Oh, Madame,' she whispered, and buried her face in her hands, sobbing out of control.

Wordlessly, Madame let her cry. It seemed to Lelia she would never be able to stop, but finally she did. She wiped her eyes and blew her nose on her tissue.

'I'm so sorry,' she said. 'I don't know what came over me.'

'Don't you?' Madame asked in a dry tone. She reached across the table and took Lelia's hand. 'Why don't you tell me about it?'

The words came pouring out then, her marriage to Armand, his death, the way Michael had come into her life, her response to him, and, finally, the bitter sense of loss now that he was gone. When it was over, she felt better than she had in weeks, cleansed and purged somehow now that she had shared her burden.

For a long time Madame was silent. Then she said, 'Do you love him?'

'Yes,' Lelia said without thinking. 'Of course I love him. But I loved Armand, too.'

'How old was Armand when you married him?'

'Twenty-two.'

'And Mr Fielding is—how old? Thirty-four, thirty-five?'

Lelia nodded. She didn't understand. What did age have to do with it?

'Listen to me, Lelia. Armand was a pampered boy when you married him. Michael is a mature man. When he says he wants you to belong to him, he doesn't mean the same thing Armand did. Think for a moment of the patience he has shown. He has proved he doesn't want to take anything from you by force. On the contrary, he is giving you enormous power over him. Don't you see the difference?'

Lelia thought this over. 'You may be right,' she said at last in a dull, hopeless tone. 'But it's too late.'

Madame cocked an eyebrow. 'Is it? He's a proud man who has humbled himself to you time after time. I agree he won't come to you again. But what's to stop you from going to him?'

Lelia could only stare at her as a little flicker of hope flared up in her heart. 'Nothing,' she whispered at last. 'Nothing at all.'

Later that afternoon, Lelia walked slowly up the path to the front door of Michael's house on Dauphine Street. Her heart was pounding so wildly she seriously worried that she'd faint before she reached it.

After her talk with Madame that morning, she had debated with herself for hours. She knew now she loved Michael in a way she had never loved Armand. Then, she had been a timid, inexperienced girl who had been bowled over by Armand's aristocratic charm. Now, she was a grown woman who had proved she could make a life of her own. If Michael rejected her now, she wouldn't blame him, but she would never forgive herself if she didn't at least make the attempt to get him back.

She stood at the front door, trying to screw up her courage to ring the bell, when it suddenly flew open and Karen Swenson appeared on the other side.

A deep despair filled Lelia's whole being. Her heart sank. Had she come too late?

'Hi, Lelia,' the blonde girl said cheerfully. Then she stared at her, taking in the hesitant manner, the flushed cheeks. 'Come in,' she said briskly. 'I was just leaving.' She opened the door wider and numbly Lelia stepped inside. 'Michael,' Karen called over her shoulder, 'someone to see you.' She turned back to Lelia. 'Sorry, I've got to run. I have a plane to catch. It was nice to see you again.'

With that, she was gone. Lelia closed the door softly behind her and stood there rigid, listening to the silence of the house. Then she heard footsteps from the back of the house, and in a moment Michael was walking towards her. He stopped short, not five feet from her, and stood there, staring at her, his arms folded across his chest.

'Hello, Lelia,' he said at last in an even tone.

'I. . .' she faltered. 'Karen let me in. She said she was just leaving. I hope I didn't interrupt anything.'

He raised an eyebrow and began walking slowly towards her again, the dazzling blue eyes never leaving her face. He stood directly before her now, almost touching.

'As a matter of fact,' he said coolly, 'Karen just quit her job.'

'I see. I'm sorry.' Had they had a lovers' quarrel? she wondered.

'I am, too. I hate to lose her. But I understand that her

marriage comes first.' There was a note of bitterness in his tone.

She shot him a quick look. Was the bitterness directed at her, she wondered, or at the fact that he was losing Karen?

There was a long silence. Then he asked softly, 'Why have you come, Lelia?'

She looked at him. His expression was unreadable. He didn't seem glad to see her. Had she been wrong to come? As she stared, the blue eyes seemed to take on a deep gleam. A muscle twitched at his temple.

Suddenly, she didn't care if she made a fool of herself. If he rejected her, if he wanted Karen, it was only what she deserved for the way she had treated him. All she knew was that she loved him.

She lifted her chin and took a deep breath. 'I came to tell you, Michael, that I love you and want to marry you. Unless you've changed your mind.'

For a moment he didn't speak. Then she saw the gleam in his eyes grow brighter and he took the last step towards her.

'Changed my mind?' he breathed, reaching out for her. 'Never.'

Two weeks later, Lelia woke up for the first time beside her sleeping husband.

It was not quite dawn, and the room was dimly shadowed. They had been married quietly the day before at the Basilica, with only Charles and Madame Fiorini in attendance, then gone straight to Michael's house afterwards.

Slowly, now, so as not to disturb him, she rose up on

one elbow and glanced over at him. He was lying on his back, one arm flung over his head, the other at his side. The dark hair was tousled, and with a secret smile Lelia recalled how her hands had raked through it last night and held it to her breast.

A slow pulsating warmth stole through her as she thought about their wedding night, and her eyes travelled now over the still, uncovered form of her husband and at the bedclothes that had been tossed aside during their lovemaking.

Her hands ached to reach out and slide over those wide shoulders and hard chest, the flat stomach and strong, firm thighs. But she was still a little shy and didn't want to waken him.

Carefully, she raised up into a sitting position and watched him sleep, feasting her eyes on his masculine beauty. She had no idea he was awake until she heard his voice, low and teasing.

'Good morning, Mrs Fielding. Enjoying the view?'

Startled, her eyes darted to meet his. She put a hand to her mouth, mortified. The blue eyes twinkled mischievously, and he smiled, deepening the little lines at the corners. When he saw her distress, his face grew serious, and he reached out a hand and ran it soothingly over her arm.

'Hey, darling, it's all right. It's legal.' He grinned again. 'I'm not shy. I like to look at you. Why shouldn't you look at me?' The grin broadened. 'You can even touch if you like.'

'Oh, Michael,' she protested, reddening, 'you're embarrassing me.'

'You'll have to get over that,' he said firmly. The hand

slid up to her shoulder and slipped the thin strap of her nightgown off it. 'Besides,' he said in a low voice, 'that fetching outfit you have on doesn't leave much to the imagination.'

The hand moved now to cup her breast over the sheer material. She sighed deeply at his touch and looked down into his eyes, the blazing blue darkened now with passion.

'Did I hurt you last night, darling?' he murmured, the magical hand moving slowly across to her other breast. 'I guess I should have known, but somehow it didn't dawn on me that you were quite so untouched.'

She shifted her weight now so that she was leaning over him, wanting to reassure him. 'Just a little,' she said. 'I expected it to be worse.'

His arm went around her neck now, and he pulled her down on top of him, his hands trailing over her back, her waist, her hips. He kissed her deeply, then held her tightly to him, his mouth at her ear.

'I'll make it up to you,' he breathed. 'I want you to enjoy it as much as I do. I love you so much.'

Lelia clung to him wordlessly, her love for him welling up in her heart so powerfully that tears came to her eyes. Through the thin silky material of her nightgown, she could feel his hard arousal and knew that Madame had been right when she had reminded her of her own power over him.

He rolled her over on her back and pulled the nightgown over her head. Then he ran both his hands down the length of her body, from her shoulders to her knees. His mouth followed, under her ear, on her neck, her mouth, the cleft between her breasts, and back up to cover one taut thrusting nipple, then the other, until she writhed and moaned beneath him, her eager hands making their own feverish exploration of his hard muscled body.

This time there was no pain, only a mounting tension, a roaring in her ears, an explosion, and wave after wave of ecstasy rippling through her, like the aftershocks of an earthquake.

They lay, spent, in each other's arms afterwards for a long time, then slept again briefly. When Lelia awoke, she found the blue gaze firmly fixed on her.

'Well?' he asked, smiling. 'Better?'

'Mm,' she murmured, nestling closer to him, her head on his shoulder.

'Good,' he said. His head fell back on the pillow and he stretched lazily. 'It gets better all the time.'

Lelia felt a little stab of jealousy at his remark. He had known so many other women. Was he comparing her to them? For the first time since the day she had gone to his house to tell him she'd marry him, she thought of Karen.

Why had she been there? What had their relationship been? She tried to tell herself it didn't matter now, that Michael loved her, was married to her, but the nagging thought persisted.

Then Michael spoke, breaking into her troubled thoughts. 'Why the frown, darling?'

She hadn't realised it had shown on her face, and she forced a smile, intending to lie to him, to reassure him. Then she thought, I can't do that. It's wrong. I don't have to lie to Michael to spare his feelings the way I did Armand.

She put a hand up and ran it over his rough unshaven

cheek. 'I was wondering about you, Michael.'

'What about me?' he asked. He brought the hand to his mouth and kissed the palm. 'I'm ecstatic, besotted, overjoyed at my good fortune. What more can I say?'

'You're not disappointed, then?'

'Disappointed! Far from it.' He raised up now and gave her a penetrating look. 'Hey, what's all this about?' She turned her head on the pillow, but he reached out and took her chin, forcing her back to face him. 'Tell me, Lelia. Don't start keeping secrets.'

She debated another second, then plunged ahead. 'All right, then. I was wondering about the other women in your past. About Karen, especially,' she added in a small voice.

He opened his eyes wide in amazement. 'Karen! Karen was nothing to me.'

'I thought. . .' She broke off. 'You know what I thought. You were together so much, you seemed so close.'

'Only professionally and as friends,' he said firmly. 'She and Gary were having problems for a while and she needed a shoulder to cry on. Finally, she realised she'd have to choose between her marriage and her job. She chose her marriage, with my blessing, I might add, even though I hated to lose her. She was good at her job.'

Lelia sighed happily. That was all right, then. 'I'm sorry, Michael,' she said. 'I had to know.'

'Well, now you do.' He leaned over and kissed the tip of her nose. 'I told you once I hadn't lived a strictly celibate life, but from the moment I first saw you, no other women existed for me. I fell hopelessly in love with you the day I met you, and that love never wavered. Not even when you sent me away.' He smiled at her. 'Twice.' He kissed her hard. 'You're stuck with me now, Mrs Fielding, for life.'

For life, she thought blissfully. All doubts were gone now, and she moved joyfully into his waiting arms.

SOMETHING OLD,
SOMETHING NEW,
SOMETHING BORROWED,
SOMETHING BLUE

Four short stories all featuring one aspect of this
traditional wedding rhyme have been specially
commissioned from four bestselling authors and
presented in one attractive volume for you to enjoy.

SOMETHING OLD
Mary Lyons

SOMETHING NEW
Valerie Parv

**SOMETHING
BORROWED**
Miranda Lee

SOMETHING BLUE
Emma Goldrick

Available July 1992
Price: £3.99

Accept 4 FREE Romances and 2 FREE gifts

FROM READER SERVICE

An irresistible invitation from Mills & Boon Reader Service. Please accept our offer of 4 free Romances, a CUDDLY TEDDY and a special MYSTERY GIFT... Then, if you choose, go on to enjoy 6 captivating Romances every month for just £1.70 each, postage and packing free. Plus our FREE Newsletter with author news, competitions and much more.

Send the coupon below to: Reader Service, FREEPOST, PO Box 236, Croydon, Surrey CR9 9EL.

NO STAMP REQUIRED

Yes! Please rush me 4 Free Romances and 2 free gifts! Please also reserve me a Reader Service Subscription. If I decide to subscribe I can look forward to receiving 6 brand new Romances each month for just £10.20, post and packing free.

If I choose not to subscribe I shall write to you within 10 days - I can keep the books and gifts whatever I decide. I may cancel or suspend my subscription at any time. I am over 18 years of age.

Ms/Mrs/Miss/Mr _____ EP30R

Address _____

_____

Postcode_____ Signature _____

Next Month's Romances

Each month you can choose from a world of variety in romance with Mills & Boon. Below are the new titles to look out for next month, why not ask either Mills & Boon Reader Service or your Newsagent to reserve you a copy of the titles you want to buy — just tick the titles you would like to order and either post to Reader Service or take it to any Newsagent and ask them to order your books.

Please save me the following titles:		Please tick √
PAST LOVING	Penny Jordan	
WINTER OF DREAMS	Susan Napier	
KNIGHT TO THE RESCUE	Miranda Lee	
OUT OF NOWHERE	Patricia Wilson	
SECOND CHANCE FOR LOVE	Susanne McCarthy	
MORE THAN A DREAM	Emma Richmond	
REVENGE	Natalie Fox	
YESTERDAY AND FOREVER	Sandra Marton	
NO GENTLEMAN	Kate Walker	
CATALINA'S LOVER	Vanessa Grant	
OLD LOVE, NEW LOVE	Jennifer Taylor	
A FRENCH ENCOUNTER	Cathy Williams	
THE TRESPASSER	Jane Donnelly	
A TEMPTING SHORE	Dana James	
A LOVE TO LAST	Samantha Day	
A PLACE OF WILD HONEY	Ann Charlton	

If you would like to order these books from Mills & Boon Reader Service please send £1.70 per title to: Mills & Boon Reader Service, P.O. Box 236, Croydon, Surrey, CR9 3RU and quote your Subscriber No:..(If applicable) and complete the name and address details below. Alternatively, these books are available from many local Newsagents including W.H.Smith, J.Menzies, Martins and other paperback stockists from 14th August 1992.

Name:..

Address:..

....Post Code:........................

To Retailer: If you would like to stock M&B books please contact your regular book/magazine wholesaler for details.